Cocoa & Carols

A Wilton Hills Christmas

Marianne Rice

Published by Marianne Rice, 2019.

Dedication

For my hot cocoa, fuzzy sock, warm blanket, and Christmas loving friends.

CHAPTER ONE

Patrick Johnson should be used to the craziness of the holiday season by now. He'd grown up with a family obsessed with every day stamped on the calendar. Groundhog Day, Earth Day, Cinco de Mayo. Heck, even Boxing Day. Who cares that they lived in Wilton Hills, Maine? Might as well prepare a huge meal and celebrate with the Canadians.

The first day of spring meant the annual family shopping trip to the local nursery to pick out flowers and bulbs, even though their little town was usually still buried in snow. Labor Day weekend, his mother turned the front porch into a fall festival with bales of hay, pumpkins, and mums. And the day after Thanksgiving all the Christmas decorations went up. His family would be busy tomorrow—if not tonight—lugging totes of decorations from the garage into the house. Patrick's mother—and father, for the most part—found any reason to decorate, celebrate, and make a meal together.

"Officer Johnson," Tonya from dispatch called on his radio. "We got another call about that suspicious vehicle. This time it's parked at Three Pines Farm."

A parked car at Three Pines was odd since they were closed and the owners were down south for the winter. Saving the reports he'd been working on, he closed his computer files and shrugged on his coat. "I'm on my way, Tonya," he said into the two-way radio before clipping it on his belt.

The police station wasn't as large as some others in the state, and they handled only the towns of Wilton Hills, Hockett, and Westwood, just west of the more upscale town of Kennebunk. With only him and four other officers on the force, there was a good chance he was working a holiday.

And since he and Brent were the only two not tied down with a wife and kids, they usually traded off. Working the early shift on Thanksgiving wasn't too bad. It got him out of preparation duty and not having to bring anything for the dinner. Not that his mom or sisters would want him to after working a twelve-hour shift.

Cooking genes were spread pretty evenly among the Johnson siblings. His sisters loved all aspects of cooking and baking, while he and Hunter preferred the cooking part. And even more the eating part.

Patrick zipped up his coat and tucked his cap under his arm as he headed out to his cruiser. The bitter cold smacked him in the face. You never knew what weather you were going to get for Thanksgiving in Maine.

Some years it topped fifty and others they were hit with a blizzard. This year was cold and dry. No snow yet, but with temps hovering in the twenties at four o'clock in the afternoon and threatening to dip to the single digits overnight, he was sure Mother Nature would be brutal come December.

He didn't wait for his cruiser to warm up and made the short drive to Three Pines. It was the largest farm in the area with a sizeable parking lot to host events from strawberry and blueberry picking in the summer to apples and pumpkins in the fall. They'd closed up two weeks ago and wouldn't open again until early spring.

The out-of-place aging dark blue Honda Civic was the only car in the vacant lot. With the Monroes gone, the neighbors made it their duty to keep an eye on the place. The Monroes were a hardworking bunch who never took a day off and supplied nearly half the county with fresh fruits and vegetables. Not only that, they were good people.

The lights to Patrick's cruiser shone on the empty car. Not even five and already nearly dark as pitch. Turning off his engine, he settled his service cap on his head and made his way to the car.

Flicking on his flashlight, he peeked inside. Boxes and totes filled the back. A pile of blankets occupied the front passenger seat. He scanned the area. Not a sign of anyone.

He placed a hand on the hood of the car. *Cold.* Whoever the owner was wouldn't be gone for too long in this weather. He called the New York license plate into Tonya and asked her to run a scan.

While he waited for her report, he headed toward the farmhouse to make sure the owner of the Civic wasn't making him or herself too comfortable inside.

A few minutes later, after checking all the exterior doors and windows, he deemed the house as empty as the lot.

"Officer Johnson, you there?" Tonya called on the radio.

"Ten four, Tonya. What'cha got for me?"

"The owner is Jocelyn Grace Redding. Last known address was an apartment in Brooklyn, New York. She's currently employed by the Kennebunk Playhouse. No known residence since July."

"She must be living with friends or family."

"I can keep digging if you want me to."

"No. She hasn't done anything wrong." *Yet.* Who knew what she brought into their small Maine town from New York? He'd heard about and seen his fair share of drugs crossing into their state. If that's what this Redding woman was doing, he'd gladly escort her to a jail cell and then back to New York.

Not that he wanted drug trafficking there, but definitely not here under his watch, near his people.

"Ten-four," Tonya signed off and he made another trip around the locked car. With no probable cause, he couldn't exactly open and search, but he could wait for her.

Finally, after his toes had nearly frozen in his boots, a dog barked in the distance. A few minutes later, a woman appeared walking said dog.

As soon as she clearly noticed him, she stopped moving, her head lifted, and her torso straightened. The dog's tail wagged furiously and it let out a *yip*. Not a large dog, but sometimes the littlest ones were the nippiest.

Patrick waited for her to come closer to the vehicle and then called out in a greeting. "Evening." Or rather, afternoon. The dark sky made it seem much later than it was. "Are you lost, ma'am?"

"Um, no." She wore a dark green winter hat with a pompom on the top, a thick coat, and a puffy purple scarf. From what he could see, she had fair skin and stunning cheekbones.

Really, Patrick? Surprised at himself for noticing such a ridiculous thing, he dropped his gaze to her dog. Tan with floppy ears. A beagle mix, he guessed, a female. He crouched down and gave the anxious pup a pat on the back. Her tail wagged, and she lifted her front paws onto his knee and licked his face.

"Cocoa, down." The woman, Jocelyn, pulled the dog away. "I'm sorry about that. She's overly friendly. Her only switches are on and off. She's been cooped up in the car so much—"

As if realizing she'd said too much, she stopped talking and took a step back.

"I noticed the boxes. Moving in?"

"Um, no. Not exactly." She kept her gaze from his and lowered her head as if hiding something.

His first impression wasn't that she was on drugs. But that didn't mean she didn't have any in the car. Or a weapon.

"You do know you're on private property?"

"I am? Oh, I'm so sorry. I'll leave." She went to the passenger side, unlocked it, and let her dog in.

"Where are you heading to tonight? Family?" It was Thanksgiving after all. Most likely she was coming or going to someone's table.

"No. I—" Again she stopped herself. "I'm sorry for trespassing. I'll be on my way." She slid into the driver's seat and started her car.

It wasn't like she'd done anything terribly wrong. Patrick had no reason to continue questioning her or to believe she was up to no good.

Still, his police instincts couldn't help but kick in. He watched as she backed out of the lot and turn left onto the road.

JOCELYN LET OUT A SIGH of relief when she'd made her fourth turn and had yet to see headlights in her rearview mirror. The officer was nice enough, but he freaked her out a little. He was right. She had been trespassing.

She was surprised it took three days for someone to report her car parked at the farm. She'd visited there frequently last month, walking Cocoa along the trails and eating the fresh apples from the trees. Not the ones hanging from the trees, which weren't many by the end of October. Instead, she'd helped herself to the drops that often went forgotten.

Many were picked up and turned into cider, pies, and other treats, but there were too many for the farmhands to keep up with, so it wasn't exactly stealing. She hoped.

Two weeks ago, when she'd stopped by to walk the trails again, the sweet farm owner had told her they were closing up and would be taking their annual trip to South Carolina to stay with their family for the holidays.

That's when her idea formed. For three days she had a steady place to stay and hadn't lived in fear waking up every twenty minutes. Granted, she and Cocoa weren't exactly comfortable sleeping in the car so she didn't make it past a solid hour of uninterrupted sleep anyway. She turned the car on every two hours, on the evens. Midnight, two, four, and six in the morning.

After their early morning walk, she'd leave the lot and drive to a busier parking lot where she could get lost in the crowd, and no one would notice her hanging out in her car. The nights had been the hardest, moving from lot to lot while wanting to be safe and undisturbed.

The little money left in her bank account needed to be saved, rationed to cover the cost of food and gas. Hopefully by spring she'd have enough saved to rent an apartment. The money she'd made acting in the off-Broadway musical this past year had barely been enough to keep up with the monthly payment on her sister's medical bills.

Next to her, Cocoa barked, taking her mind off her past. The comforting sound somehow managed to elicit a smile on her lips.

"I know, girl. But we won't have to live like this for much longer. Promise. You like Three Pines Farm though, don't you?" Yesterday morning they came across a deer in the woods.

Noticing how quiet it was, Jocelyn drove around the quaint town of Wilton Hills. Everyone was spending the evening with their friends and family, enjoying Thanksgiving turkey, watching football, talking about their plans for the holidays.

She glanced over at Cocoa, her constant and only companion. "I'll make sure Santa visits you too, baby."

She easily found a spot to park on Main Street. Geesh, it was like a scene right out of a movie. Cute shops decked out in Christmas decorations already lined the narrow road. Each lamp post had a wreath attached, and according to the fliers posted around town, the big tree in the park would light up tomorrow night.

The street wasn't long, less than a quarter mile. She and Cocoa got out and strolled down the empty sidewalks, peeking in the windows of the storefronts—a bakery, an insurance company, a convenience store of sorts, gift shops, clothing boutiques, an art gallery, and at the end, a music store.

She spent the longest time gazing in the window of *Key Notes*. A baby grand piano sat in the front corner, and a bookshelf that seemed to go on forever filled with music lined the side wall. She avoided the store when it was open. Too tempting to spend the little money she had on new sheet music.

Besides, she could find most of it online and print it at the library. With no phone, no computer, no Internet, the library was her favorite place to hang out. If only they'd allow dogs inside, she could spend more time there.

As the days grew colder, she couldn't leave Cocoa in the car for long, and it was getting harder to find places where she could bring her. Jocelyn's fingers grew cold, despite her wool mittens, so she returned to the car and drove around searching for a place to park for the night.

Since the town seemed fairly dead, she figured it would be safe to stay at the small town park. No need to set her alarm every two hours. Either she or Cocoa would wake from shivering. After she fed Cocoa and let her do her business by some trees, they climbed back into the car.

"Ready to cuddle?" Jocelyn climbed over into the passenger seat and wrapped her and Cocoa in four blankets. She checked the time before shutting off the car and laughed. "Six o'clock. Really? It feels like midnight."

She couldn't wait for warmer, longer days. By then she hoped she wouldn't still be sleeping in her car. She opened the book she'd borrowed from the library and set up her flashlight so she could read for a few hours.

She'd read only two chapters when Cocoa stirred in her lap. "I know, baby," she cooed, rubbing her face against her puppy's face. Cocoa's body shook and then she let out a loud *yip*.

"Easy girl."

Something tapped against her window and Jocelyn let out a loud screech. "What the..." Her heart leaped into her throat and she wrapped her arms around Cocoa for comfort.

A light shone outside, followed by a deep voice.

"Miss Redding?"

No one knew her around these parts. She wasn't far from Kennebunk where she'd been hired to play a small role in *A Christmas Carol*, but what person would be walking around at this time of night who actually knew her name?

"It's Officer Johnson. We met a few hours ago."

Ohnoohnoohnoohno. She couldn't afford any trouble with the law, not that she'd ever been in trouble before. Unless he knew about all the times she'd trespassed. But that was just to walk Cocoa or to find a place to park for the night.

Unless he was there to arrest her for all the apples she'd eaten and hadn't paid for. And the raspberries. The berries were amazing.

"Miss Redding?" He tapped again.

She couldn't roll down the window without turning on the car and didn't want to open the door, bringing in more cold air than necessary. Reaching over the shifter, she started the car and rolled the window down a few inches.

"Hi, Officer. I was just, uh, reading a book." Which was totally true.

"Are you okay, ma'am?" He flashed his light in her backseat and then returned it to the front dash, politely not pointing it in her eyes. Still, the night was too dark for her to make out his features, not that they were hard to remember.

Sharp cheekbones, jet black hair that curled slightly from under his cap, concerned eyes, and shoulders that probably had trouble fitting through doorways.

"Just fine, thank you. It's a really good book and I, uh, must have gotten so caught up in the story that I lost track of time."

"Ma'am, do you have a place to go?"

"Sure. As soon as I finish this chapter I'll be on my way." Cocoa whined from under the blankets.

"Ma'am," he said again, making her feel a hundred instead of thirty-one.

Given the events of the past year, she felt a whole lot older. Gone were her days of fun-filled energy. If she didn't have Cocoa to keep her moving, she was afraid she'd have lost her spirit as well.

"There's a women's shelter in Portland. I can contact them to see if they have a free bed tonight."

"Oh, no. I wouldn't want to take an open bed away from someone who needs it." Which was true as well. If she needed to, she could find a place that would give her a room for really cheap. It would mean she would fall behind with her sister's medical bills, but she wasn't as down and out as many others.

"Miss Redding, you can't sleep in your car. You'll freeze to death. As will your dog. Why don't you follow me back to the station and I'll see what I can find for you?"

"I don't—"

"I can follow you in your car, or you can come in mine." The sternness in his voice told her he wasn't accepting no for an answer.

"I'll follow you."

He gave her directions. The station was only two miles from the park. No wonder he'd found her so easily. She got out of the passenger seat, rounded her car, and climbed behind the wheel.

Before she could close the door, he put his hand on it, stopping it, and said, "I'll follow *you*."

They soon reached the station. Hoping he'd let Cocoa come with her, she attached the leash and patted her thigh. "Come on, baby. We're going to get warm."

Officer—Johnson he said his name was? —waited for her by her car.

"Come on inside. I can't promise the coffee's the best you'll have, but it'll warm you up. Sergeant Richardson brings his German shepherd to work sometimes. I'm pretty sure there's a bag of dog food in the back."

He disappeared and came back a minute later with two bowls. He set them on the floor in front of Cocoa, who wagged her tail and lapped up the water and food in seconds. Jocelyn had been monitoring the bagged dog food in her trunk, rationing it as much as she could without starving her dog. So this extra meal was a welcome bonus.

Whatever brand this was, it was obviously tastier than the generic stuff she'd been feeding Cocoa.

"Thank you. I can pay your sergeant back for the food."

The officer scrunched his brows and shook his head. "He won't mind. Trust me."

"Hi, Patrick. I thought I heard you come in the back. Oh, hi." A middle-aged woman wearing a headset and a smile greeted her, then noticed Cocoa. "Oh, isn't she adorable? What's your name, honey?"

"That's Cocoa."

"Speaking of, I'll get you a cup of coffee. How do you like it?" Officer Johnson asked.

"Black is fine, thank you." Cream and sugar were extra luxuries she couldn't afford right now, but since he was offering.... "Actually, cream and sugar, please."

"There's still some of May's apple pie in the break room. Can I get you a piece of that, hon?" The woman asked.

"Oh, no. I couldn't—"

"She'd love one," the officer interrupted. He eyed her again with the scrutiny of someone who didn't trust much and turned on his heels, disappearing around the corner.

"I'll be right back." The woman left as well and Jocelyn found herself alone.

She'd never been inside a police station before. It wasn't what she'd expected, what she'd seen on television and in movies. It shared the same building as the Town Hall, which didn't appear to be much larger than the station.

The front door had led them to an open room with four desks, one door that apparently led to an office, and another door leading to what she presumed to be the break room, since they'd both disappeared behind that door.

The tiled floors were industrial looking while the walls and window trim matched the character of the old building.

"Here you go," the officer said, returning with her coffee. "You can have a seat over here if you'd like." He stacked two folders on a desk and pushed aside a pile of papers to make room for the pie the woman had just brought.

Just as she took a seat, a new voice rang out. "Happy Thanksgiving," the officer said. A rush of cold air accompanied his words. "What are ya still doing here, Johnson? I thought you were on your way out thirty minutes ago. Figured you'd be shoveling turkey down your throat by now."

"I got a bit sidetracked."

The officer glanced at Jocelyn and a wry smile escaped his lips. "That so?" He crossed the room, took off a glove and held out a hand to her. "Any friend of Patrick's a friend of mine. Brent Dwelley, nice to meet you..."

"Um, Jocelyn. Jocelyn Redding." She stood and shook his hand. "But I'm not—"

"Cute dog." Brent crouched to rub Cocoa behind the ears. "You going over to Patrick's folks for Thanksgiving?"

"Oh—"

"Actually." Officer Johnson moved between them and cupped his hand under her elbow. "She is." Cocoa, the traitorous pup, *yipped* again and rushed up to him, nudging her nose into his leg. "And so is Cocoa."

"Oh, I—"

"The alternative"—he turned to face her and lowered his voice— "is a warm meal at the shelter." His dark, chocolaty eyes bored into her. Instead of smiling and friendly like she'd expect from a man inviting her to Thanksgiving, he was broody. Stubborn, for sure.

"Your family..." His wife, not that he was wearing a wedding band, but that didn't mean he wasn't married. What family would welcome in a stray to their table on Thanksgiving?

"The more the merrier is my mother's motto. After dinner I'll make sure you and Cocoa find a warm place to stay."

Dangit. He didn't appear to be any happier about the invitation as her, but she accepted anyway.

She turned to the nice woman. "Thank you for the pie," she said, even though she never had a chance to take a bite. It was nice nonetheless.

"Sure thing, *Jocelyn.*" There was a slight edge to her voice as if she and the officer—Patrick—were in on something. "Enjoy your meal, you two."

Yeah, the glint in his eyes, the faint trace of a smile worried Jocelyn just a tad.

CHAPTER TWO

What was I thinking? He wasn't, that was the problem. Patrick held the door open for Jocelyn and waited for her and her dog to step through. When she headed for her sedan, he reached for her arm and stopped her.

"You can ride with me."

"I can't put you out anymore, Officer. Your offer was kind, but I can't impose on your family. Especially last minute."

She was right. He needed to let his mom know to set a plate for one more. She'd already held off eating until six. Taking his cell out of his pocket, he groaned. *Seven.*

When he'd driven by Jocelyn's car at the park and saw a faint light from inside, he turned around to make sure she was okay. As he expected, she was homeless and too proud to check into a shelter.

Part of him couldn't blame her. A young, pretty woman in a shelter would be prime material for any shady characters. The volunteers who ran the homes in Portland were top notch, and as far as he knew, there were very few reports of abuse there. But still...

He dialed his mom's number and kept his eyes steady on Jocelyn. "Hi, Mom."

"Patrick. Is everything okay? We're holding dinner for you."

As he knew she would, unfortunately. Guilt for always being the one to mess up family meals crept up his spine.

"Sorry to hold you up. You know you guys could have started without me. Thanksgiving leftovers are just as good."

"I've been doing my best to keep your brother and Liberty from picking all the pecans off the sweet potato pie."

It was his favorite and they loved to taunt him by eating more than their share of the topping.

"I'll be there in fifteen minutes. And, uh, I'm bringing a... friend with me, if that's okay."

"Of course it is. I'll set another plate." As he knew she would.

He pocketed his phone and opened the passenger door of his cruiser for Jocelyn. He waited for Cocoa to jump onto her lap before closing it. He had no idea what he was doing or why he thought to invite Jocelyn to his parents' house. His sisters were going to razz him no end. Hunter would probably chime in when he wasn't busy chasing little Georgia around.

Starting up his cruiser, he took a moment for it to warm up and to give Jocelyn a heads up about his family.

"My family is loud, nosy, and they love holidays. Like holiday overkill. At least my mom's like that. And pretty much my three sisters. My dad, brother, and I just go along with the flow."

"Wow. You have a big family." She stroked the dog's ears. "That must have been nice growing up together."

"It had its moments." He put the cruiser in reverse and backed out. "Another fair warning, we haven't had a dog in years."

"Oh, I can stay with Cocoa in the car." At the sound of her name, the dog turned her head toward Jocelyn and licked her face.

"I didn't invite you over so you could sit in the driveway. I invited you to get you out of the cold." Yes, that was the only reason, he told himself. It had nothing to do with her gentle voice and those hurting eyes. It wasn't like he was a sucker for a woman in peril. He'd never done anything like this before.

She didn't say anything the rest of the way to his parents' house. Once there, he parked his cruiser behind the four other cars that crowded the driveway. Jocelyn met him at the front of the car, Cocoa attached to her leash.

"My niece and nephew are going to be all over her." He pointed to Cocoa. "How is she with kids?"

"She hasn't been around many, but the few times they've come up to her at the park she's been very friendly. I can keep her on her leash. Or in the garage."

"No. My family wouldn't allow that. My sister April is a veterinarian. She'll be fighting the kids for the dog's attention." They'd end up spending the entire night in the garage so they could play with her. "Come on." He didn't mean to sound so gruff, but he wasn't looking forward to the wrong impressions they were about to give.

She waited by his side while he grabbed his bag from the trunk. April had the door open, a hand on her hip. "It took you long enough. Oh! You brought a dog." She pushed him out of her way and crouched in front of Cocoa. "Oh, aren't you a pretty girl. You're so happy to see me, aren't you, girl?"

"Told you." He turned to Jocelyn and laughed. "Take no offense that she hasn't noticed there's a human attached to the leash."

"I saw her," April said from her crouched position. "Mom said you were bringing a *friend* to dinner. Figured you'd rather have me playing with your new four-legged friend than drilling your new friend with questions."

She was correct on that account.

"I'm April, by the way." She stood and gave Jocelyn a hug. "Welcome to the crazy."

Patrick studied Jocelyn to see how she'd react. For whatever reason, he was interested in her. Maybe it was just in the story he was sure she was hiding.

"Thank you for having me. Us. I'm Jocelyn and this is Cocoa."

"Welcome. Now come on in. It's freezing out here." April took off toward the kitchen.

They rushed through the door, and he waited by the front closet while Jocelyn unbuttoned her coat. She gnawed at her bottom lip before slipping off the coat. "I'm not exactly dressed for Thanksgiving dinner."

He took in her jeans, sneakers, and plain gray sweatshirt. Even dressed casually, she was pretty.

"I'm going to have serious hat head." When she pulled off her hat, her hair stuck up in a rainbow of static.

"Don't you hate that?" Liberty came up behind them and brushed Jocelyn's hair down with her hands and gave her a hug. "I'm Liberty, the favorite sister. April says you're Jocelyn. 'Bout time my knucklehead brother brought home a nice girl."

"You're a far cry from my favorite." He gave her a hug and kissed the top of her head. No way was he responding to her comment about bringing home a nice girl.

Jocelyn hovered in the corner of the entryway, her arms crossed over her chest, looking nervous and out of place. He handed Liberty their coats and stood between them in an attempt to give Jocelyn a moment of privacy.

"It's okay," he said softly. "I know they can be overwhelming, but no one is judging you based on your outfit. My sisters will probably change into leggings or sweats before dessert."

"What's the matter?" Always nosy, Liberty shoved her way between them.

"I didn't exactly give Jocelyn much notice about dinner." He could have at least asked her if she needed anything out of her car, but it wasn't like he was checking out her clothes. She hadn't even taken off her coat in the station. The jeans were fine, but he could see why she was self-conscious in her sweatshirt.

His sisters were wearing nice sweaters and pants. His mother would be wearing one of her holiday blouses, and his father and brother would have on button downs. Just as he would be as soon as he changed out of his uniform.

"Of course you didn't. My brother has no clue about women." Liberty tapped her finger to her chin and looked Jocelyn up and down. "We're about the same size. I have a few backup outfits in my car if you want to borrow something."

As a journalist, she never knew when she would be called to a job, so she kept spare outfits on hand.

"You're too kind, but I couldn't do that to you."

"Do what?" Liberty said, oblivious to her situation. "Give me a sec." She was out the door before Jocelyn had time to protest.

"Hi, honey," his mother said from behind him. He turned and hugged her, then introduced her to Jocelyn.

"It's so nice to meet you." In Johnson form, hugs were given around, even from his father who joined the party in the entryway.

Liberty came barging back in. The front door smacked him in the back.

"'Kay, man of steel. Maybe you could work out a little more." She pretended to check the door for dents, and he rolled his eyes at the overused joke.

"Uncle Patrick!" His favorite nephew called from the kitchen.

"I tried to hold him back as long as I could so you'd have time to catch your breath," his sister Noel said, her belly just showing her pregnancy.

Gabe crashed into his legs and Patrick hugged the nine-year-old. "Hey bud. You still growing? I swear, you're going to be taller than me before you hit double digits."

"That's what Mom says too." Gabe's mother had died when he was only three, and all he had left of her were pictures. When Ian and Noel married earlier this year, she'd officially adopted him, but he'd been calling her Mom since they'd gotten engaged.

"Happy Thanksgiving, Noel." He hugged her and shook Ian's hand, pulling him in for a man hug and pat on the back. "How're her cravings?"

"Hopefully not as bad as Maria's were." Hunter's yell from the kitchen was followed by an "Ouch!"

Patrick turned around to introduce Jocelyn to the rest of the crew, but she and Liberty had already gone upstairs with the change of clothes. His mother looped an arm through his and guided him to the kitchen. Uncertain about leaving Jocelyn, he looked over his shoulder.

"She'll be fine. She's in good hands," his mother said.

"I wouldn't call Liberty good hands," April teased as she set a heaping bowl of potatoes on the counter.

They often ate buffet style for the holidays. There wasn't much space left to add more to the two tables pushed together, but his mother had reset the table so Jocelyn had a place.

"Gabe made place cards for everyone." She held up a turkey in the shape of Gabe's hand. "We brought extras in case one got broken but it doesn't have her name on it." Noel made the perfect second-grade teacher. She loved arts and crafts, and more importantly, kids, and was excellent at her job.

Once a year he visited her classroom and talked about stranger danger and let the kids sit in the back of his cruiser, telling them it better be the only time they find themselves in the backseat.

"She'll appreciate it. Already she feels like she's intruding."

"Obviously she hasn't met our family yet, or she'd know there's no such thing."

"Give her time. It took me three days being trapped here to realize that," Ian teased.

"Hey." Noel swatted him with a towel.

It had taken Patrick more time than that to fully trust his now brother-in-law. A wicked storm may have stranded Ian alone with Noel in the house for three days, and she had said he'd been a perfect gentleman, but it took more than Noel's word for Patrick to soften and trust the man. Ian was as solid and honest as they come, and Patrick was happy for his sister.

In his line of work, he knew better than to trust so easily.

"I'll be right back." He held up his gym bag and made his way down the hallway into the guest bedroom to change. Not wanting Jocelyn to come downstairs and him not be there, he hurried, stumbling with the top two buttons on his shirt.

"Thanks, you guys, for waiting for me. For us," he said when he returned a minute later.

"Not gonna lie," Hunter said, picking up a roll and tearing into it. "I've been picking at that turkey for the past forty minutes. You're serving up last, little brother."

"Okay, we're ready. Let's dig in," Liberty called as she walked through the living room into the crowded kitchen.

Jocelyn had changed into a thin purple sweater that looked like it was made for her. It accented her shape instead of boxing her out like her sweatshirt had. She still wore her jeans, and her dark hair fell softly around her shoulders and looked smooth as satin.

An unfamiliar feeling churned in his stomach.

Hunger pains. Had to be. He cleared his throat. "For those of you haven't met her yet, this is Jocelyn. Uh, that's my brother-in-law Ian, my nephew Gabe. Georgia is..."

"She and Maria are upstairs dealing with a timeout. My daughter inherited her aunt Liberty's temper."

"Hey."

"True," Maria said from the hallway, Georgia resting on her hip. "And she has the Johnson charm to go with it. Somehow she talked me out of a timeout and into reading her four books instead."

"Great. We've done the rounds. Anyone else who hasn't met Jocelyn yet can do so once we've served ourselves. I'm starved. Thanks, Mom, for this amazing meal." Hunter took Georgia from Maria and handed his wife a plate. "Serve up now before Miss G here needs to be chased around the house."

The men stood back while the women took plates from the stack at the end of the counter and served themselves. Normally Patrick would go last, especially since he held up another family meal, but his brother nudged him ahead so he could be behind Jocelyn.

Once seated elbow to elbow, they bowed their heads while their father said grace. It was short and sweet, and all were relieved when they could dive in. Jocelyn sat to his right, her leg and arm bumping his often.

It wasn't her fault he took up so much space. He'd always been a big guy and spent a lot of time staying in shape. She was a petite thing, frail, and almost timid looking, yet he'd seen a spark in her eyes when he'd shined the light into her car and denied the offer of a bed at the shelter.

A few minutes into their meal, when the hunger pains had subsided, three conversations took place at the same time, in usual Johnson fashion.

"So where did you two meet?" his mother asked Jocelyn.

Nearly choking on his stuffing, he took a sip of water to wash it down and answered for her. "We, uh, met at Three Pines Farm."

Out of the corner of his eye, he could see relief on her face.

"We used to take the kids there every year to pick strawberries, blueberries, and apples. Isn't it a beautiful farm?"

"It is." Jocelyn used her napkin to blot her mouth. A pretty mouth. "I take Cocoa for walks down the trails. I hear they'll be opening up for cross-country skiing after Christmas so we'll have to find a new area to walk."

"Do you live nearby?"

A question Patrick was curious about as well. According to what Tonya found in her quick search, Jocelyn hadn't had a legal place of residency in four months. Picking up on her nervous gestures—squirming in her seat, taking another sip of wine—he changed the topic.

"How's construction going?" he asked Ian.

"Slow. We're hoping to get the roof on before the first snowfall." They'd bought land not far down the road and were running into one delay after another.

Conversation turned toward Ian and Noel and their hopes to have the house completed before the baby came in May.

"Do you know what you're having?" Jocelyn asked.

"Not yet." Noel rubbed her belly. "The big day is coming up in a few weeks. Ian and I are still arguing about it." She elbowed him in jest.

"I want to be surprised," he said, rubbing his side with a smile.

"I want to plan."

Knowing his sister, she'd get her way.

"We should plan one of those gender-reveal parties," Liberty said. "Where you like, open a box and either blue or pink balloons come out."

"Like luck of the draw? How are they going to know what color balloons to put in the box?" Patrick snorted at the silly idea.

"Seriously. You're so clueless." April tossed a pea, hitting him squarely between the eyes. "They'd have to let someone know the sex of the baby, and then that person would plan it. Noel, let me, please?"

"No fair. I want in," Liberty whined.

"What about me?" Maria added. "I'm the one here with the most recent pregnancy experience."

"I'm the grandmother," his mom added.

"Or we could just wait until the little nugget comes out." Ian laughed. "See? Much easier."

"We'd have to have someone else know, so it would be fair." Noel's eyes grew big with excitement. "Jocelyn. You could do it."

"What?" Her fork clanked onto her plate.

Patrick cleared his throat as he thought of a way to steer the conversation away from her again.

"Sure. You're now a friend of the family. I'd trust you not to spill the baby beans to my sisters. Could you keep the secret from Patrick?"

She tapped a finger to her lips as if in deep thought, contemplating how close he was to Jocelyn.

"I'm... I'm honored but I... I don't—"

"Let's take it one day at a time," Patrick said, interrupting. "Besides, Ian hasn't even agreed to wanting to know the baby's gender."

"Party pooper." He got another pea between the eyes, this time from Noel.

Relief set in again when the conversation turned toward Gabe, who kept them entertained with stories from school. They all helped themselves to seconds. And thirds. Especially Patrick. He worked a thirteen-hour day on little food.

Besides, he worked most of it off at the gym and volunteering at the after-school program at Wilton Hills High.

When everyone had their fill, he, his brother, and father got up and started clearing dishes. Ian picked the turkey filling containers with meat, and Hunter put the food away.

"What can I do to help?" Jocelyn asked.

"Nothing. We're stereotypical around here. Girls cooked so the boys clean."

"But I didn't do anything to help."

"Doesn't matter." April looped her arm through Jocelyn's and pulled her toward the living room where his sisters and mother would relax and entertain the kids for a few minutes while the men cleaned up.

"She seems nice," his brother said, handing him a plate to load in the dishwasher.

"Yeah." She did. Quiet and reserved, which he could totally understand. Being homeless and suddenly invited to a stranger's house for Thanksgiving would do that to a person.

"I like her," his father said, patting him on the back. "It's good to see you with a nice girl. Been too long since I've seen that kind of look on your face."

"What look?"

His father scratched his cheek as if trying to figure out the right words.

"Content. Happy. Still young, this relationship with you two, I'd guess."

"Dad." *What?* What could he say? That he'd discovered Jocelyn living in her car and offered her a seat at their table? It was the truth, but he didn't want to humiliate her. Not that his family would ever intentionally make her feel uncomfortable. If anything, they'd smother her more, offer her a place to stay, three home-cooked meals a day, and then some.

From the little he knew about Jocelyn, which was nothing, she was embarrassed about her situation and didn't want handouts. Not even from the homeless shelter.

"Ah, baby bro's in love and is trying to play cool."

Patrick scooped up a handful of bubbles and flung them at Hunter. Let them tease and taunt him about his new *girlfriend* as long as they didn't make her uncomfortable.

Laughter from the other room caught his attention. Not only the normal sounds he was used to from his family, but the unfamiliar sweet sound of Jocelyn's laugh.

It sang through his body and wrapped around his heart, giving it a little squeeze. This wasn't supposed to happen. She wasn't supposed to fit in so well with his family.

She wasn't supposed to take up space in his heart.

CHAPTER THREE

Jocelyn hadn't laughed this hard since she and Kimmy went on their final sister trip together to Miami two years ago. They spent their days lounging on the beach and their nights experiencing the exciting nightlife, dancing and laughing until the wee hours of the morning.

The trip took its toll on Kimmy, but she insisted on going. Not for her, but for Jocelyn. At the time they hadn't known it would be the last time Kimmy would go anywhere other than her apartment and the hospital.

"How could he not know his dog was pregnant?" Maria swiped her eyes, still laughing.

"I don't know. That little schnauzer's belly was ginormous. She pushed out six puppies in my waiting room and Mr. Donner just stood there screaming like the clinic was on fire."

Jocelyn scratched Cocoa's belly. "That's too funny. He didn't even help? Just stood there and watched?"

"Yeah." April snorted. "Donner has to be at least eighty. You'd think in all his years he'd have a clue about the birds and the bees. The look on that man's face... it was like Pookie was spitting out gremlins instead of puppies."

"Pookie?" Liberty laughed.

"He got her from the shelter a few years ago and didn't want to change her name."

"I thought about changing Cocoa's name too." At the sound of her name, the sleeping pup lifted her chin off Mrs. Johnson's lap.

"What would you have named her?" Noel put her feet up on the coffee table.

"It sounds silly now." Jocelyn rubbed Cocoa behind the ears.

"Tell us," several voices pleaded.

"My sister and I never had a dog growing up." Well, they sort of did.

It depended on the foster home they were in and how long they stayed there. They'd made a pact when she was twelve and Kimmy was eight that they'd get an apartment together in the city and have a dog. Jocelyn would be starring in a Broadway musical and Kimmy would be a hot-shot attorney.

"When we were kids, we said one day we'd own a chocolate Lab and name him Aladdin after our favorite movie."

They spent hours and hours coming up with the three wishes they'd say when they rubbed their magic lamp. Finding Prince Charming was always at the top of their list.

"Oh, I love that movie too. Maybe I'll add Jasmine to our girl list."

"And start a Disney theme instead of a holiday one?" Liberty picked up the bottle of wine and held it over Jocelyn's glass.

She covered it with her hand. "No thank you. I'll be driving later." Not far. The park was only a few miles from the police station where she left her car. Still, two glasses of wine in one night was plenty. A luxury she hadn't experienced in ages.

Liberty filled Maria's glass and added only a splash to her own. "In case you didn't pick up on it, our mother named the five of us kids after holidays or seasons."

"My birthday is the obvious one," Noel said.

"Christmas Day?"

"Christmas Eve."

"Fourth of July here." Liberty waved like a princess on a float.

"I'm the mistake."

"April." Mrs. Johnson sighed. "She surprised us by being nearly two weeks late. I already had blankets embroidered with her name on it."

"May second baby." April held up her water glass in a salute.

"Hunter's an October baby. I contemplated naming him Jack but he arrived in the first half of the month. Since Alex is a hunter, it seemed fitting."

"And Patrick's birthday must be March seventeenth?"

They all cocked their heads slightly as if surprised she didn't know his birthday. She'd been on plenty of dates with men, even third dates, and didn't know their birthdays, so it shouldn't come as a surprise.

"It is." April tucked her feet under her and played with Cocoa's tail. "So tell us again how you and our surly big brother met."

He'd done an excellent job running interference at dinner. Anytime his family asked a personal question, he redirected the conversation. Whether it was because he was embarrassed at bringing a homeless person to dinner or an attempt to save her dignity, she didn't mind. She was grateful whatever the reason.

"We've only... seen each other a few times." Twice. Tonight. Both times he'd warned her about trespassing or the dangers of sleeping in her car. Not exactly a first date.

"Well, sometimes you know when you know. Ian and I fell in love after three days together."

"Ugh. Our sister the romantic. Did Patrick tell you about that story?" Liberty asked. Jocelyn shook her head. "Two years ago, a wicked storm kicked Maine's butt. Ian and Gabe's car crashed into the tree out front. They were stranded in the house with Noel with no power until we all came to their rescue on Christmas Eve."

"And they lived happily ever after," Mrs. Johnson added.

Jocelyn would love to hear more of the romantic tale. They seemed incredibly happy and in love, Ian and Noel. And Gabe was adorable as well, vying for attention from his aunts, grandmother, cousin, and now Cocoa.

"What's your love story?" she asked Maria.

"Nothing as fairytale as Noel's." She set Georgia down and watched her as she rushed to Cocoa. "Gentle, sweetie."

"She's fine. Cocoa loves children."

"Georgia can be a bit rough at times. Anyway, I met Hunter when I was temping at the bank. He swept me off my feet with his charm."

"Our brothers are anything but charming. Did you ever hear about the time Hunter—"

"Lies. They're all lies." Hunter came in the room, chucking Liberty on the back of the head. He took a seat on the arm of Maria's chair and kissed her temple. "I can't speak for Paddy, but I definitely inherited the Johnson charm."

The rest of the men joined them in the living room and their conversation turned to three simultaneous ones. Pie, more laughs and stories, and soon Jocelyn found herself getting too comfortable. It wasn't right to make this nice family think she deserved to hear their stories.

"Miss Georgia is going to be a bear tomorrow if we don't get her home and in bed." Maria scooped her up while Hunter got the coats and diaper bag. "It was nice meeting you, Jocelyn. I look forward to the next time."

Hugs made their way around the room, and then Ian and Noel collected their coats. "Sorry gang. This little one and this big one—" she rubbed her belly and then Gabe's head "—have me tuckered out as well."

When it was down to just Patrick, his sisters, and parents, Jocelyn waited for him to say they were leaving as well.

"Let's play a game." Liberty dropped a stack of games on the coffee table. "Pictionary or Taboo?"

"It's getting late," Patrick said from the archway between the living room and kitchen. He'd changed into a navy button down and khakis earlier, and she struggled not to gush. He was imposing in his uniform and in normal people clothes... breathtaking in an overwhelming way.

There was... a lot of him. She supposed he had to stay in shape to do his job but... wow. It was a wonder he could find a shirt that had sleeves to fit around his arms and would button across his wide chest

"Oh, don't be a party pooper."

"Some people actually worked today." He headed toward the coat closet but April spoke up as well.

"Come on, Paddy. One game. Jocelyn doesn't even look tired. You didn't work today, did you? We didn't even ask what you do."

"Oh, I—"

"Enough with the interrogating."

Kind, but Patrick really didn't need to come to her defense. She actually had a job. Not a high paying one, but one that helped her with Kimmy's medical bills. "I'm working at the Kennebunk Playhouse."

"You're an actress? How exciting." Mrs. Johnson would find a grocery store cashier exciting. The woman was adorably sweet.

"Sort of. Singing is actually what I prefer to do but there aren't many musicals this time of year. I'm the back-up ghost of the future. It's a musical rendition to *A Christmas Carol*." It was what had lured her here. That and the fact that she got the part.

New York was too cut throat. She'd tried her hand in Philly and Boston, but that wasn't much better. Without a fancy degree or some serious name dropping, she was just another résumé.

When the small playhouse in Kennebunk called her in for an audition in last month, she jumped at the chance. Really, though, she'd take a job at the local grocery store if necessary. It was her fallback job for January. That or waitressing.

"Cool." Liberty opened the Pictionary box. "What else have you starred in?"

Starred in? Nothing. So far all her roles had been minor. She was waiting for her big break to come. One day it would, she prayed.

"Just odds and end roles. I haven't played Pictionary in ages," she said hoping they'd pick up on the change of subject.

"Can you draw as well as you can sing?" April snagged the pad of paper and handed out pencils.

The Johnson family was like that, assuming she was good just because she said she liked to do it. If she was that great, she wouldn't be living in her car.

"I'm not terrible."

"You're on my team. Patrick's a terrible artist. You don't want to pair with him anyway, but you probably already know that."

"I'm no worse than you." Patrick joined them, taking a seat on the couch next Jocelyn. "You sure you want to play or are you ready to get going?"

Going? Where to? She'd stay in the warmth and comfort of the Johnson home forever. She glanced at Patrick next to her on the couch. She'd noticed how big he was the first time she saw him standing beside her car.

When they sat next to each other at dinner, his thigh brushing up against hers, and his elbow occasionally bumping hers, followed by a soft apology, she couldn't help the blush. Or the butterflies in her belly.

At first, she connected it to hunger pains, but she wasn't starving. One good thing about working at the Playhouse was they always had food out to snack on. And they didn't mind Cocoa being inside. Two good things. Three, considering she got paid to sing.

"If you're tired..."

She wanted to stay, really wanted to stay, but it wasn't fair to Patrick asking him to stay late after working a long day.

"It's okay." His gaze was gentle. And knowing, as if they had a secret between them, which they did. Only she hadn't told him. But he'd figured it out all on his own.

"Do you really stink at this game?"

An adorable grin escaped his lips. "Guess you'll have to wait and find out."

"Sweet. You and Lib and me and Jocelyn. We're gonna kick your butts."

"You're not playing?" Jocelyn turned to Patrick's parents.

"Oh, we know better than to get involved. We sit back and watch the show," Mrs. Johnson said.

"We jump in to referee when needed. This will be an experience for you." Mr. Johnson chuckled, patting his wife's hand.

An hour later, Jocelyn's ribs hurt from laughing. "What is that?" She and April could barely see through their tears as they watched Patrick attempt to draw for Liberty.

"A shoe. No, a horse. A candy cane!" Liberty shouted.

Patrick frowned and growled. Yeah, the man growled a lot at his sister. "Where the heck do you see a candy cane?"

"Hey, no talking," April reminded him.

Liberty was doing the best she could. Whatever it was that Patrick drew could only be described as something between a... shoe, a horse, and a candy cane. Jocelyn laughed again.

"Time's up." April tossed the timer in the box. "What the heck is that?"

"It's a reindeer."

If she squinted really hard she could almost make it out.

"Georgia can draw better than that," Liberty whined.

"You're not much better." Patrick handed the notepad to Jocelyn. "Here you go, Picasso. I'm pretty sure you hustled us."

Since he was a police officer aware of her living conditions, she thought he was serious at first, but the glint in his eyes told her otherwise. Accepting the compliment, and the paper, she drew a card and grinned.

Less than a ten seconds later April shouted, "*Star Wars!*"

She hadn't realized they were sitting so close until Patrick shot to his feet, nearly knocking her over.

"Are you serious? You couldn't guess reindeer in three minutes and April can get *Star Wars*."

"You probably already know this, but our brother is a sore loser."

"Not exactly fair when you have Jocelyn on your team. Next time she's with me." Liberty tossed the timer in the box.

"Next time she's with *me*," Patrick corrected.

Her heart skipped a beat and she chewed on her bottom lip. Did he mean...did he mean...?

He glanced down at her, his mouth open in surprise. No, apparently he didn't mean there'd be a next time. It was just a knee-jerk response to his sisters. Jocelyn got that.

Standing as well, she made her way to the stairs. "Is it okay if I go upstairs to change? I need to give you your clothes back, Liberty. Or I can take wash them and... give them to Patrick to return." She'd been a regular at the laundromat in Westwood, not that she had many clothes to wash.

"Not worried about it." Liberty fluttered a hand at her. "Just bring them the next time we get together."

Patrick gave April a nudge with his foot, and she scrambled to her feet. "Can I talk to you for a sec?" April asked. She steered Jocelyn toward the kitchen and down the hall to the spare bedroom.

"So, Patrick talked to me earlier." Closing the door behind her, she clasped her hands together and then spread them out.

Uh oh. "About?"

"He didn't tell me much, just that you're sort of without a place to stay right now."

"Yeah. Sort of. It's okay though. I've got things figured out."

"You're more than welcome to stay with me. I have an extra bedroom in my duplex. I've actually been looking for a roommate, but the right one hasn't come along."

"That's kind of you to say, but you don't need to go to the trouble."

"No. Seriously. I have." She took her phone from her back pocket and clicked on an app. "See?"

April handed the phone to her and Jocelyn read the ad. She really was looking, but the rent was way more than she could afford.

"I'm surprised you and Liberty don't live together."

"Ha! Never. We'd eat each other alive."

Jocelyn handed her back the phone. "It's kind of you to offer but—"

April put a hand on her arm. "Think of it as a free trial period. Bunk with me this weekend and by Monday, if we're ready to tear each other's hair out, you can find somewhere else to live. If we end up liking each other more than we already do, then we'll figure something out."

"I couldn't take advantage of you like that."

"I don't see how it's taking advantage. I literally have a room that's not being used. I mean, if you're a hot water hogger and leave me with a cold shower every day, we'll have to end this relationship sooner rather than later." April hugged her.

"How do you know I'm not some terrible person who's going to steal your stuff?" Unfortunately, she spoke from personal experience. There were too many horrid people out there. Her last roommate left her pretty scarred.

"Because my brother wouldn't have brought you here tonight. He's never done that before, brought a woman he was seeing to a holiday meal. A backyard barbecue maybe, but not often. He's a good judge of character."

Maybe he was, but that wasn't the situation with them. Tonight, he'd had the holiday spirit in him and offered a homeless woman and her dog a free meal.

"You'll stay? Just the weekend? Then I reserve the right to kick you to the curb Monday morning."

It really was a tempting offer, and she wasn't exactly looking forward to sleeping in her car tonight.

"Cocoa..."

"You know I'm a vet, right? I'd have a houseful of dogs if my job didn't require me to work such long days."

"Your landlord is okay with having a dog there?"

"Do you really think I'd be renting from a place that wasn't pet friendly? Come on. Let's go back to my place, roomie." She looped an arm with Jocelyn's and led her back to the living room.

April nodded to Patrick who seemed to sigh in relief. Another good deed for the night. The man was surely going to heaven.

"I'll drive you to get your car," he said as he helped her with her coat.

"Did you meet him at the station?" April asked, ignorant of how they really met.

"Yes."

"You've had a long day, Paddy. I'll take her and then she can follow me."

He looked like he wanted to argue with her, but he closed his mouth and nodded. A smile lit April's face. "Unless you two want some alone time before she comes over. It wasn't exactly like you had any tonight."

"I'm sure they'd appreciate a few minutes of quiet," Mrs. Johnson said from behind them, wrapping her arms around Jocelyn in a hug. "It was lovely to meet you. Please don't be a stranger."

"You're welcome here anytime." Mr. Johnson hugged her too. She envied how free they all were with their hugs, not caring if they'd known you for a minute or their entire lives. They made her feel special when she was...no one.

"Nice meeting you, even if you totally scammed me and brother here out of the game." Liberty hugged her. "Oh! What's your cell number? We should get together for lunch sometime."

"I don't have a phone."

"Really? How do you function? I mean, I'd be lost without mine."

"You're stuck to yours twenty-four seven. It would be good for you to step away from it from time to time."

"It's my job, Dad. I never know I'll get called to a breaking story."

"She's staying with me for a few days so at least you know where to find her." April shrugged into her coat.

"Why do you get her? She can stay with me if she needs a place to crash."

"We have three spare bedrooms as well," Mrs. Johnson added.

Feeling uncomfortable with the offers, she buttoned her coat to her neck and ducked her head.

"Chill, guys. Give her some breathing room." Patrick draped his arm around Jocelyn's shoulder and guided her to the door. "Thanks for everything, Mom and Dad."

"Oh, the leftover pies. Take them with you." Mrs. Johnson dashed off toward the kitchen.

There'd been eight pies, plates of cookies, and a cheesecake. More than enough left over for them all to have one.

"I'll take the pecan." Liberty snagged it before anyone could argue.

"Here's your Dutch apple, Patrick." Mrs. Johnson added to Jocelyn, "I always make two, knowing he'll want his own to take home."

"What's your poison, Jocelyn?" April asked. "I love anything pie so we can't go wrong."

"I'm not picky. Everything you made was delicious."

"Why don't you take the chocolate cream then?" Mrs. Johnson said. "It'll save me from polishing it off on my own since Alex doesn't care for it."

"Not when there's lemon meringue and pumpkin to choose from," Mr. Johnson said.

"I'll come by after work tomorrow to help decorate," Liberty said.

"If I do it won't be until late," April said.

"Don't count on me. Sorry, Mom." Patrick gave her an apologetic hug.

"I miss the days when you all weren't so busy," Mrs. Johnson said with a heavy sigh. "Your father will have to pull double-duty filling in for you kids. I'll save some ornaments so you can decorate the trees the next time you come over."

After another round of hugs, they left, waving goodbye to the parents.

Patrick's cruiser was parked behind April's black SUV, and he followed her to the passenger side.

"I'll start the car. Don't mind me." April slid behind the wheel and a moment later the car engine started.

He tucked his hands in his pockets and stared at her as if searching for the right words. Clearing his throat, he opened his mouth, shut it, then crouched down to rub behind Cocoa's ears.

"She's a good dog. Everyone loved her."

"She loves people."

Patrick stood and tucked his hands back in his pockets again.

"Thank you for everything you've done for me tonight. Bringing me here, asking April to open her guest room to me. I appreciate it. You went far above the call of duty. You're an excellent police officer."

Because why else would he do so if he hadn't been on the job when he found her in the parking lot?

"I... you're welcome."

"I guess I'll see you around." She shrugged. "Maybe." After Monday she'd be searching for another place to park her car at night. She promised herself when the temperature dipped below zero, she'd splurge and rent a cheap motel room. Knowing Maine's reputation for cold winters, she'd be spending a lot of money on motels.

She opened the car door, and Cocoa didn't waste a second to get out of the cold. She hopped inside and made herself comfortable in the passenger seat.

"I had fun tonight."

"Me too. And your sisters are right, you're a terrible artist." That earned a grin.

"Maybe sometime you can teach me how to draw."

Her brows lifted in surprise. "Maybe." Most likely not. It was a kind thing to say. That same knee-jerk reaction as earlier tonight. "See you around."

She slid in the car, moving Cocoa to the side and then placing her on her lap.

"Buckle up. And drive safely."

"Yes, Officer Johnson," April said, tooting the horn as she maneuvered her car around his cruiser.

"My brother is totally smitten with you."

"I wouldn't call it that."

"Oh yeah?" April chuckled. "Then what?"

Obligated? No, he hadn't been obligated to bring her to his parents' home. Polite for sure. It was quite obvious his parents had instilled manners and generosity in their son. He had no interest in Jocelyn otherwise.

But the little shivers that ran through her body when his quiet smile was directed at her gave her a glimmer of hope to hang on to.

Hope for what, she wasn't sure.

CHAPTER FOUR

H e had no reason to be so... obsessed with Jocelyn. Sure, she was sweet. Sure, she was kind. Sure, she was beautiful. But he'd met plenty of other sweet, kind, beautiful women before.

Patrick parked his cruiser in the driveway in front of the right side of his rental duplex. Two cars were parked on the left, Jocelyn's and April's. Would Jocelyn have agreed to stay with April if she'd known he lived right next door? It wasn't like he was stalking her.

However, when he glanced into the front window on his way up the walk to his front door, he had to question whether he was.

No. Definitely not. He often checked on his sister when he came home, or at least checked to make sure she was home safe every night. With Jocelyn—and Cocoa—safe and secure inside a warm home tonight, he could go to bed with a clear conscience.

Even if she didn't have dark eyes that sparkled when she laughed, and a smile that made her whole face glow, he would've still felt guilty leaving her to freeze in a parking lot. Especially on Thanksgiving.

His original intent wasn't from interest in her as a woman but as an officer looking out for the people in his town. Even if she wasn't technically part of his town, she still deserved a warm meal and a shelter warmer than her car.

Patrick let himself into his apartment and tossed his keys on the table by the couch. Tempted as he was to call his sister or to knock on her front door, he resisted and made his way to the kitchen and stored the chocolate cream pie in the fridge.

With another long day on tap for tomorrow, he chucked his shoes over by the back door, made sure it was locked, and then headed upstairs.

THE SUN HADN'T MADE its way up yet and already Patrick was awake. And not by choice. Turning over, he pulled his pillow over his head and tried to block out the unfamiliar sound.

"Come on, Cocoa, it's freezing out."

Jocelyn. Like a fish swimming toward a worm on a hook, he leaped out of bed and peered out the window.

Yeah. Totally not a stalker. It was too dark to see anything anyway, so he backed away from the window and slid on a pair of jeans and a sweatshirt. He rushed down the stairs and turned on the kitchen light. After momentary blindness, he blinked to help his eyes adjust before going to the back door.

As he opened his door, the one next to him from April's back deck shut. Backing away and hoping no one witnessed his stupidity, he closed his door and leaned his back against it.

What was he thinking? That he'd have a casual conversation with Jocelyn at five-thirty in the morning in zero-degree weather? Now that he was up, he made a pot of coffee and took out ingredients to make a breakfast sandwich.

Thirty minutes later, he was fed, dressed, and warming up his cruiser. Jocelyn's car was no longer in the driveway. Sometime while he was in the shower she'd left. April's was warming up, the frost nearly gone from her windows.

"You're up early for working the long shift yesterday," April said as she locked up her side of the duplex.

"I was up so I figured I'd hit the gym before work."

"Yeah. All that food yesterday is going to your gut." She patted his flat stomach and gave him a kiss on the cheek. "Thanks for suggesting Jocelyn stay with me. I hope she likes it here, and it becomes permanent."

"That would be good." His words formed a puff in the cold morning air.

"Unless." She cocked her head and gave him a stern looking. "You break her heart. Then she'll want to move. If you do, you're the one moving out. Got it, bro?"

"I don't plan on breaking her heart."

"Well, to be fair, I don't think most people ever *plan* on breaking someone's heart. I like her. She's cute and silly. Be good to her." With a pat on his cheek, she got in her car and sped off.

Silly. Jocelyn was silly. Yeah, he could see that. She fit right in with his family last night, giggling and cracking jokes, even if he was the butt of them.

Chuckling, he warmed up the cruiser. Not wanting to wait for the defroster to kick in, he reached for the scraper in the back seat and chiseled away at the frost and ice on his windows. A few moments later, he drove away.

After consuming so many carbs yesterday, he spent a little extra time on his cardio workout before hitting the weights. It wasn't vanity that kept him in good shape, but a respect for his job. Not that all police officers needed to be as strong as he was, but it was one thing he could offer to his community. He saw the way people, women especially, felt protected and safe with him there.

Wilton Hills and the neighboring towns were relatively safe, not to say there wasn't the ne'er-do-well who caused a ruckus that he had to take care of. Unfortunately, many of his calls were domestics. Walking into a dispute, he never knew what he'd find. Maybe someone armed and dangerous, drunk, high on drugs, filled with rage and ready to take on anyone in sight.

His size and strength came in handy and he used it to his advantage, making women and children feel safe, not dominated.

After his gym workout, he pulled into the station and put in a full uneventful twelve hours of work. Most wouldn't complain about that.

Hours of paperwork, a few hours of patrol, and a few more hours of paperwork, and he called it a day.

Back at home, when he didn't see Jocelyn's car, he knocked on his sister's door and let himself in. Cocoa greeted him with a sniff at his pant legs. He bent down to scratch behind her ears.

"I regret the day I gave you a key," April called from the kitchen.

"It wasn't locked." He'd told her over and over again to always lock her doors, even when she was home. Especially when she was home.

"You slumming for a meal? Mom brought leftovers." Funny. She didn't give him any. April laughed at his scowl. "She came by the clinic this afternoon with them. I'm pretty sure she wanted to get the scoop on you and Jocelyn, but I was super busy. I can't tell you how many dogs got into turkey carcasses last night and this morning."

"Cocoa was okay?"

"She's adorable. I told Jocelyn I'd take her to work with me. You should have seen her. So good. She didn't bark or snarl at any of the other dogs or cats. She's such a people pup."

"Where, um, is Jocelyn?"

April glanced down at the dog and then back at him with a smirk. She scooped up some kibble from a bag and poured it into Cocoa's dish. "Don't tell me you suggested she stay here so you could keep tabs on her."

"No. Not at all." He prayed she didn't think that. "She doesn't have a phone and I..." He what? Even if she had a phone, he doubted she'd have given him her number. It wasn't like that with them.

"So how do you guys connect? With her not having a place to stay and no phone? Are you so in love that you have telepathic powers?"

"Funny."

Cocoa crunched on her food.

"I'm heating up a plate. Want some?" April took three containers out of the fridge and set them on the counter.

"No. That's for you and Jocelyn."

"She won't be home for dinner. I think she said the last show is over close to nine."

"Show?"

"Seriously. Guys are the worst. Do you even listen to her when she talks to you? She had a noon, three, and seven o'clock performance today."

Scrooge. How could he forget? She'd briefly mentioned her job last night. Of course she'd be busy with the Christmas play now that it was officially the holiday season.

"I knew that." He checked the time on his watch. The show had already started but maybe he could get there in time to see the second half. That's when the Ghost of Christmas future appears anyway. "Enjoy your dinner. Lock up behind me."

Patrick kissed her on the cheek and gave Cocoa a quick pat before he rushed out the door.

The parking lot to the Playhouse was packed. He found one spot at the far end and wedged his cruiser between a Suburban and the fence. Zipping up his coat as he jogged down the lanes of the lot, he wished he'd had enough common sense to wear a hat and gloves.

Jocelyn did that to him. Made him forget his sense. Not that it was her fault.

"I'm sorry, sir, but the show is sold out," a woman in the lobby told him.

He unzipped his coat and tucked his hands in his pockets to warm them up.

"Oh. I'm sorry, Officer. Did you need to—"

"No." He held up his hand realizing he never even changed after his shift. "I'm off duty. No official business tonight. I'm actually—" *What the heck. In for a penny—* "I'm here to pick up—to meet Jocelyn Redding."

The woman, Peggy, according to her nametag, smiled. "Oh, she's a sweetie, that one. We were lucky to find her last minute. Roger says he hopes she auditions for the spring play as well. We're doing *Mary Poppins*. Wouldn't she be an excellent Mary?"

Yeah, he could see that.

"Is it okay if I wait here?" It beat waiting in his car. How Jocelyn thought she could survive sleeping in her car he hadn't a clue. Unfortunately, there were far too many people in worse positions than her.

"Sure. Can I get you a cup of coffee? We have leftover snacks back in the dressing rooms."

"No, thank you. I'll be fine."

It was another forty minutes before the play ended, and a rush of people filled the lobby. Polite husbands and boyfriends left to warm up the cars while the women and children stayed inside. That was nice to see.

A few couples went out together, and one woman left while her significant other stayed behind. It wasn't until Patrick noticed the walking cast on the man's left foot that he took back his negative thoughts about him.

"Do you need any help getting to your car?" he asked the man.

"My sister is taking care of me, but thank you, Officer..."

"Johnson." Patrick held out his hand and shook the man's. "That's awful nice of your sister to be supportive."

"I don't know what I'd do without her. Her husband, sorry SOB if I ever met one, took off with the little she had in the bank account. At least he left the kids with my baby sister. She's a good mom. Even looking out for her older brother now."

"Family is important. I'm glad you two have each other in a time of need. If her husband ever comes back and stirs up trouble, be sure to give your local police a call."

"Will do. Thank you, Officer.

It was a catch-22. He loved supporting and helping people, but he hated that his job was necessary. The world would be a better place if everyone would think of someone besides themselves.

Patrick saw him out and went back into the lobby to wait. When most of the crowd had left, he went inside the theater in search of Jocelyn. Two crew members, Scrooge and Tiny Tim, by the looks of them, hung out by the stage chatting with a few members of the audience.

He waited for their conversation to end, followed by a round of hugs—family and friends, he guessed—and went up to them as they were heading toward the back.

"Excuse me. I'm looking for Jocelyn. Can you let her know Off—Patrick Johnson is out here?"

Scrooge turned around. "You a friend?" The wrinkles, painted on with makeup, crinkled even more. "Family? Or on business." By the look of that scrutiny, he'd guess she didn't get many visitors.

"Friend."

"Okay. I'll let her know." Scrooge put his hand on Tiny Tim's waist and lifted him up to the stage, then hopped up and disappeared behind the curtains.

It seemed like forever before Jocelyn came out, wearing the same clothes she had on last night.

"Hi." She sucked in her lips and rocked back on her heels, seeming embarrassed by his visit.

"Hi." Now what? He hadn't thought the rest through.

"Did you, uh, like the play?"

"I didn't see it."

"Oh." Her mouth turned down.

"I didn't get out of work in time. You have more shows tomorrow, right?" He knew because he read the dates and times while he waited in the lobby.

"Yes."

"Good. Good." He followed suit and stuck his hands in his pockets. "I'll get tickets to the next show."

"I can give a ticket. Two if you wanted to bring...a date or someone."

The only date he'd bring was her and since that wasn't possible, he came up with the next best date. "My family would love to come see you." They hadn't talked about it, but they'd be thrilled to see Jocelyn perform.

"They don't have to do that."

"Have to? You met my family."

That earned him a grin. "April said she wanted to come. I gave her two tickets to tomorrow's two o'clock performance."

"Perfect. I'm not working. I'll finagle a date with her."

"Jocelyn, do you want to come to dinner with us tonight?" One of her castmates called out as they walked through the other side of the theater.

She looked to Patrick and then back to the four who had congregated by the door. "Um, not tonight, guys. Thanks for the invite though."

"Next time, okay?"

"Sure." She seemed hesitant and he'd bet his badge she often declined the offer. They left, loud laughter in their wake.

"I don't mean to keep you from your friends."

"No, it's okay. I wasn't planning on going out anyway."

"Have you been here since this morning?" He doubted she'd taken time to eat anything all day.

"We had one last rehearsal before our noon show."

"You must be starving."

"There were snacks in the dressing rooms."

"How about a late dinner? Sounds like the rest of your crew was hungry so you must be as well."

"I... you don't have to..."

"I know I don't have to. I want to. Besides, I haven't had dinner yet either. Can you believe my mom gave April leftovers but not me?"

"Really?"

"Keep giving me that pity party over dinner." He placed his hand on her lower back and escorted her down the aisle of the theater. "There aren't many places open this late. Pizza work for you?"

"You don't have—"

"I *have* to eat. That's a nonnegotiable." Once outside he glanced around the nearly empty parking lot until he spotted her car not far from the back entrance. "I'll wait while your car warms up. Mine won't take as long. Can I trust you to follow me to the Pizza Dome?" he said of a popular pizza joint not far from there.

"Are you sure?"

"If you're not hungry you can watch me eat. Kidding," he said, hoping his joke wasn't taken seriously. "I'd love your company and then you can tell me about the play."

"Don't tell me you've never seen *A Christmas Carol* before."

"I have but I'd love to hear you talk about it. Besides, this one is a musical. I can't say I've ever seen the musical version."

That earned him another grin.

"Okay, but don't say I didn't warn you."

JOCELYN WAS HEARTENED by Patrick's gesture. He'd come all the way to the theater to take her to dinner. As her car warmed, so did her insides. His entire family were beautiful souls, and he was blessed beyond measure to have two supportive parents and a handful of siblings.

When she spotted his cruiser in her rearview mirror, she backed out of her parking space and followed him down the road to the restaurant.

She'd declined the offer to join her castmates every night after rehearsal. Tonight's opening performances was a night of celebrating, but she'd already told them she had to get back to Cocoa, which was somewhat true.

April had been sweet to offer to take her to the clinic with her. Knowing her dog wasn't alone all day took a bit of pressure off her shoulders and enabled her to focus on her lines.

The three performances went off without a hitch. Even with her small role, she felt just as much a part of the cast as if she'd had the lead. The woman who was cast to play the Ghost of Christmas Future still had another two weeks of recovery before she could put pressure on her foot. In the meantime, Jocelyn would put her heart and soul into the role.

Turning into the lot behind Patrick, she pulled up next to him. She met him by the front entrance and when he opened the door, the aromas of garlic, basic, and tomato filled the air. "It smells delicious. I didn't realize how hungry I was." Her stomach growled.

It was a seat-yourself style restaurant so they picked a booth away from the doors to avoid the draft. "What's your poison?"

"Poison, huh? This doesn't sound like a good start to a da—" No, not a date. "I'm not picky."

She glanced up and noticed his shy smile. Maybe he did think of this as a date. Better than a pity meal. A date would be amazing. Fabulous. Spectacular. But she wasn't fooled in believing a handsome man with a solid career and loving family would out of the blue fall for a homeless woman with no future.

"No poison here. Promise. They make the best pizza around."

"Or is it that they're the only place open this late during Maine's off-season?"

"Maybe a little of both."

She looked at the menu and went for the ultimate test. "You're either a lover or a hater. What's your take on Hawaiian pizza?"

"Hot, sweet pineapple paired with salty ham covered in melted mozzarella cheese? It's like a pizza and a delicatessen all wrapped up in one. In the summer, I like to grill slices of fresh pineapple. Peaches too, drizzled with balsamic vinegar."

"That sounds amazing."

"I'll grill you some fruit sometime. You'll love it."

Sometime. Like there'd be another time like this, them enjoying a meal together.

The waitress came over and asked for their order. She asked for a water as did Patrick.

"We'll have an extra-large Hawaiian," he added as he handed her the menus.

Jocelyn rested her elbows on the table. "I never said I liked Hawaiian pizza," she said after the waitress left.

"Oh. I thought...when you said the grilled fruit sounded amazing." He scratched his shoulder and craned his neck looking for the waitress. "I shouldn't have assumed. I'm sorry."

"I'm kidding." She laughed. "Good detective skills."

He squinted at her, biting back a grin. "You had me there for a second. I don't usually order for a woman or make assumptions."

Usually. He was the epitome of a perfect gentleman in every way, shape, and form. He had to have a long line of women who waited around for a date with Officer Johnson.

"No worries. That wasn't the impression I had."

"So, tell me about the play. How did you get started in this business?"

She waited while the waitress set two glasses of ice water in front of them. When they were alone, she continued. "I've always loved to sing. I don't mind acting. It's more or less the side effect of wanting to star on Broadway."

"Broadway, huh? New York, is that where you plan on going after this?"

"That's where I'm from. Albany, really. I started out in school plays and then got a few lead roles in the local theater."

"That's amazing. I can't sing, dance, or act. I look forward to watching you tomorrow night."

"Thank you," she said shyly. "I'm no Liza Minnelli or Patti Lupone."

"The names ring a bell but I'm not familiar, so you don't have to worry about me comparing you to them."

"You have to know who Liza is." She laughed in disbelief when he shrugged his massive shoulders. "What about Bernadette Peters?"

"Maybe if I saw them in a movie. I'm more the action-adventure type though."

"Wow. You really don't know musical theater. Even Hugh Jackman has starred on Broadway."

"Wolverine? Tell me more." He leaned forward, resting his elbows on the table, and looked at her like he really was interested in knowing more.

"About Liza and Patti," she teased. "Or Hugh?"

He shook his head. "About you."

It had been a long time, a *really* long time since a man had any sort of interest in her, or rather, since she had the time or the opportunity to spend time with a man.

"You said you're from Albany. Do you still have family there?"

This was where their not-exactly-a-date could go downhill. If she ignored his questions, he'd think she wasn't interested and was being rude. If she responded, he could become *un*interested.

Since their time together was probably limited anyway, she went with the truth.

Leaning back in the booth, she let out a deep sigh as she toyed with the napkin in front of her. "My sister and I moved from foster home to foster home. It wasn't until I was a junior in high school and she was in seventh grade that we found a semi-permanent home. The Henleys took care of us for two years. Once I graduated and turned eighteen, I worked for guardianship of Kimmy."

"That must have been hard on both of you."

"It was. But it beat the alternative."

"Your foster parents, the Henleys and those before, did they..."

"Nothing catastrophic happened to us, thankfully. We fought hard to stay together. We were in and out of the system a lot in elementary school. By the time I was in sixth grade and Kimmy in third, our mother lost all parental rights. The usual. Neglect. Stupid stuff. She was young and not ready to be a mom. My sister and I have different birth fathers. Neither ever made an appearance in our lives."

She and Kimmy had never talked about their parents. They'd never been an important figure in their life. They couldn't miss what they never had.

"I'm sorry." He covered her hands with his. The warmth from his touch spread through her body, and she found comfort in the gesture.

"The summer after high school I had a job working in a bank during the week and got the lead role in *Oklahoma,* which played on weekends. I made enough to set us up with a studio apartment and frozen meals. We were living the dream." She laughed softly and he squeezed her hands.

"We did okay for a few years. Kimmy graduated from high school with high honors and got a scholarship to Hostos Community College. Tuition, room and board paid for, and if she maintained at least a 3.5, the scholarship would carry over to a four-year school."

"You must be proud of her."

"So much so." While Kimmy was still in high school, they'd had more of a mother-daughter relationship. After that, it grew into a friendship and a sister bond like no other. "She earned an associate degree in business and got accepted into Fordham. I moved to the city and did the clichéd thing. Waited tables while auditioning at every theater in the city."

"I've been to New York City only once. That place freaks me out. You two are strong women for living there. Makes me wonder how you ended up in Maine."

She pulled her hands from his and crossed her arms over her chest.

"We had a few good years, and then Kimmy was diagnosed with leukemia."

"Jocelyn." He reached for her again, but the waitress came with their pizza.

"Can I get you two anything else?" she asked as she set the large pie on the table.

"No, thank you." Jocelyn reached for a napkin and placed it on her lap. The food came at the perfect time. "This is gigantic. Don't tell me you can polish off one of these on your own."

"After a long day, sure can."

They both picked up a slice and placed it on their plates, steam and layers of cheese trailing behind.

Picking up her fork and knife, she cut off the end and blew on it before taking the bite.

"Fork and knife? I thought you lived in New York. They don't eat their pizza like that, do they?" He picked up his slice and folded it like a taco.

"No. And I only eat the end piece and only when the slices are huge so I don't have to fold my pizza like that." She pointed her fork at him and laughed.

"Mmm. Good."

They didn't talk through their first piece, but when he slid a second on his plate, Patrick sat back. "Tell me more about Kimmy."

"I thought you wanted to know more about my singing career." If she could even call it that.

"I want to learn more about you, and your sister is a big piece of your life."

Was.

"How is everything?" the waitress asked as she came by.

"Delicious, thank you," Patrick responded for them.

Jocelyn wiped her mouth with her napkin and took a drink of water. "Kimmy fought hard for nineteen months. She died last March."

"Jocelyn. I'm so sorry." He pushed their plates and the pizza to the side and took both her hands in his. "I can't even imagine what you went through. The disease and then losing her. My family means everything to me. I can't even... you must still be hurting."

This was not the response she expected to get from a man... from a man who looks like Patrick. Handsome and rugged and strong in all the right places.

The tug at her heart came from the memory of her sister and from the sympathy from Patrick.

"It gets easier but the pain, her memory, it's never far away."

His hands dwarfed hers and his fingers rested on her forearms. He squeezed and then let his fingers caress her wrists. The touch was of comfort yet it stirred up emotions and feelings she probably shouldn't be having about a man she only recently met.

Slipping her hands free, she changed the subject.

"You and your family, have you always lived in Wilton Hills?"

"My dad grew up in our house. He added the garage when we were young and cleared a bunch of trees out back so we'd have a yard to play in. My mom grew up in Portland. They met when she was working at the library, and he was studying for his chemistry final at the University of Southern Maine."

"That's adorable. Have you always wanted to be a police officer?"

Patrick bit into his pizza and chewed. When he was finished, he sipped his water and continued. "My grandfather, my mom's father, was a Portland police officer. We were close. I didn't realize how close until I graduated from high school and wasn't sure what I wanted to do with my life. Pete took me out for lunch. We talked over burgers and I thought, hey, why not? I signed up for the police academy and the rest, you can say, is history." He picked up his pizza gain.

Jocelyn followed suit taking a few more bites. The slices were larger than she was used to, and she feared she wouldn't fit into her costume if she kept eating.

"So what brought you to Maine?" He wiped his mouth with his napkin and put a third slice on his plate. The man must work out every day to burn off all the calories he consumed.

"I couldn't keep up with rehearsals while taking care of Kimmy. I was working in an off-Broadway play and was easily replaced. The city has no shortage of singers and actors."

"That's terrible."

"The show must go on." She waved her hand in the air. "I lost my enthusiasm for entertaining and needed a break. I went back to waitressing, but couldn't afford to live in the city anymore." Not after the medical bills came pouring in. "I looked for roles in Connecticut and in Boston, but those areas are also really competitive. I'd given up on singing and figured waiting tables would be my future when I stumbled across the call for *A Musical Christmas Carol*. The woman playing the Ghost of Christmas Future broke her foot riding a hoverboard, and her understudy had laryngitis. Yay me." It was only a matter of days, maybe a few weeks, before she returned to second-understudy status.

"Ouch. I can't even tell you the number of injuries reported from those things. So, when did you get the call?"

She never exactly got "the call" since she couldn't afford a cell phone, but she didn't need to remind Patrick of that. She'd used the local library's phone to call and set up an audition instead. "It was sort of anticlimactic. I came in for an audition, and they hired me on the spot. Sort of desperate, I guess. My schedule was flexible, which gave me an advantage over the others."

"You've only been in Maine a few weeks?"

"Three." Eighteen nights in her car. Eighteen too many. Before that she'd been staying in campgrounds. It was easy to find cheap state campgrounds during the summer. Many closed after Columbus Day and so her plan had been to drive south for the winter.

The owners of a small campground in New Hampshire had let her stay until November first, since Halloween weekend was their official close. They weren't open during the week but had taken pity on her and allowed her to keep her tent up on one of the sites. Between their generosity and the good tips coming in from the restaurant, she'd been able to keep up with Kimmy's bills.

The checks she got from the Playhouse would barely make a dent in the bills, but would keep food in her belly and in Cocoa's.

Patrick was polite in not asking her the obvious, *where have you been staying for three weeks?*

"Do you plan on staying in Maine when this show is over?"

No. Not if she didn't want to freeze to death in her car. "I'm not sure yet," she said instead. The logical thing to do was drive south to warmer weather where she wouldn't have to worry about sleeping in her car, and where there were campgrounds open. But if she wanted a place on Broadway, she needed to stay semi-local.

"I hope you do." He picked up his pizza and finished it in a few bites.

The waitress stopped by with a box and their bill, which Patrick quickly swept up.

"Thank you for dinner," Jocelyn said as she slipped into her coat and zipped it up.

"I ate more than my share. You can take the leftovers." He handed her the box but she held up her hands in protest.

"You paid for it, and I'm pretty sure you're still hungry. You take it for your midnight snack."

He didn't protest and held the door open for her as they stepped out into the bitter cold night.

"Thank you again for dinner. And for the company. I'm sorry I talked your ear off."

"I liked getting to know you, Jocelyn. And I bet there's a lot more to know."

Not really. She was as simple as they came. Nothing stellar about her. She unlocked her car and opened the door.

Patrick stood beside her. "Drive safely." He kissed her cheek and walked off to his cruiser.

A few minutes later they pulled into their respective driveways. When she was at her front door, she smiled at Patrick on his front stoop, less than twenty feet away. "You following me home, Officer?" she teased.

Last night, she'd been surprised when April told her Patrick was their neighbor. Knowing he was on the other side of the wall made her feel safe, and set the butterflies in her belly aflutter.

"I like to make sure my date makes it home safely." He winked at her and balanced the pizza box with one hand and fumbled his keys with the other.

His words brought a ridiculously huge smile to her lips. "I'm safe," she whispered, not loud enough for him to hear. She stepped inside and closed the door behind her.

"Hmm. Your play ended almost two hours ago, you and Patrick got home at the same time, and you have a goofy smile on your face. I'd say you had a good evening." April sat up on the couch and set her e-reader on the table next to her. Cocoa didn't even bother to raise her sleepy head from April's lap.

"I see Cocoa missed me terribly."

"I may have worn her out. Or she wore me out. Hard to tell."

"Thank you for watching her today. I owe you. For that and a lot more."

"I'd say we're even. I've been wanting a dog forever, but with my schedule I don't have time to give one all the attention it needs. I could handle a cat, but it's not the same."

Jocelyn crouched in front of her to give Cocoa some love.

"So how was your date?"

"It wasn't a date."

"Uh huh."

"He happened to be in the area and we both worked late and needed to eat."

"Right." April let out a loud laugh, jarring Cocoa from her restful slumber. "Sorry, honey." She rubbed Cocoa's ears. "My brother just happened to be...what? Walking by the Playhouse as you got out? It's not exactly in his jurisdiction."

Jocelyn thought about that. If he'd come to see the play but it was sold out, why had he stayed? Was it to see her? He was still in his work uniform so she'd assumed he stopped by on his way home from his shift. Her butterflies acted up again.

She stood and patted her leg for Cocoa to follow her. "It's been a long day. I should go."

"Hey, listen. I'm sorry for being nosy." April got up from the couch and put a hand on her shoulder. "I promise not to make it weird for you two or to pry. Please don't leave because I'm annoying. I really like having you here."

"Leave? Oh, I was just going to take Cocoa out before going to bed."

"Phew." April wiped her forehead in dramatic fashion. "I know you've only been living here for twenty-four hours, but you and Cocoa are the best roommates I've ever had."

"Wow. You must have had some pretty awful ones before."

April chuckled. "See? This is why I like you. You said that with such sincerity. Goodnight, Joce." She gave her a hug. "Can I call you that? I didn't even ask. See? Another annoying thing I do. I probably shouldn't tell you all my annoying habits, or you'll find another roommate."

As if. "You can call me Joce." Kimmy was the only one who ever called her that before. It was nice hearing it again.

"Sweet. Get your beauty sleep and rest those vocal cords of yours. I'm bringing the family with me tomorrow to check out my famous roommate."

Stage fright had never been an issue before. But knowing Patrick and his family would be in the audience added a whole new level of pressure to her job.

A pressure she found she rather enjoyed.

CHAPTER FIVE

The three o'clock show ran smoothly, as had the noon show. With only the six left, Jocelyn should have had a sense of relief, but this time the Johnsons would be in the audience. She sat at the vanity in the dressing room she shared with five other women and rummaged through the pots and jars so she could refresh her makeup.

Having the Johnsons in the audience brought back memories of when her sister and her handful of friends used to watch her. Most of the people she hung out with were part of the crew, either on the stage or behind it, so having a cheering section in the audience meant the world to her.

Not that the Johnson family would be cheering. A polite applause at the end the play most likely. April had been the most amazing room-mate treating her as if she was doing the favor instead of the other way around. Granted, she was pretty sure it was Cocoa April was so ecstatic over.

Three days ago, she never would have guessed that she'd have a warm Thanksgiving meal, be living in an apartment with a new friend, and have feelings for a man.

Wait. What? Jocelyn set down the makeup brush and blinked at her reflection in the mirror. Her cheeks were rosier than usual, and it wasn't from using too much blush. Even her neck had a pink tint.

It couldn't be...no. Patrick was just a friend. It was normal for her to feel something for the man since he'd saved her from another night of cold, uncomfortable sleep in her car and invited her to his family's home.

She was lonely, was all. Sure, he was nice. And attractive. That didn't mean anything.

Finishing her makeup, she stood and slipped into her costume. The long, heavy dress transformed her to another time period. While the long, flowing gossamer gown she wore toward the end of the play as the Ghost of Christmas Future was her favorite, the small role as a town lady was fun too. No stress about messing up her lines or singing off key.

"One more to go and then two days off. I can use it." Sarah sprayed her hair and did the same for Jocelyn. "You had a flyaway."

"Thanks."

"Any plans for Monday and Tuesday?" Sarah was a few years younger than her and a biology major. Managing rehearsals and homework was a challenge, but she said she'd been keeping up.

Jocelyn envied her ability to do both. Supporting her sister's academics and then taking care of her physically and financially when she was diagnosed with leukemia meant her education had had to take a backseat.

"No plans." Never any plans. Finding new dog-friendly places where she and Cocoa could sit inside out of the cold or discovering new parks and trails for them to walk were the only things that occupied her off-days. That and spending time at the library to look for jobs. She never stayed long, not wanting to leave Cocoa in the cold car.

"We should meet up sometime for coffee."

"Sure. That would be nice." It would. Even though Sarah was a good nine or ten years younger than her, having coffee with a friend would be nice.

A knock sounded on the door. "Show time," Gary, their producer, said.

"We're ready," Sarah called back.

THE STANDING OVATION from the crowd was like being wrapped in a warm blanket and a sipping on a steaming cup of hot chocolate while watching fluffy snowflakes fall from the sky. Warm and comforting from the inside out. This never got old. When her name was called, she stepped forward and curtsied, and couldn't help her grin when someone from the audience whistled loudly.

The curtain closed and everyone made a mad dash for the dressing rooms. Since it was the last show of the night and on a Sunday, everyone wanted to get home to their families. The weekend opener had been a sold-out success according to Gary, and they were all exhausted.

Next weekend wouldn't be as busy, but she still had a Friday night show, as well as three on Saturday and two on Sunday. That would be her routine for the next four weeks, with rehearsals on Wednesday and Thursday night. Possibly Tuesday if Gary thought they needed it.

Jocelyn didn't mind the busy schedule. She had nothing else to do and nowhere to go...until now. Sort of. It was only a matter of time until Tina got her voice back and Jocelyn stepped down to understudy.

Finding a job waiting tables at a breakfast diner would be the smartest thing to do. Not being available on the weekends didn't bode well for her though.

She still had two days of boredom, but at least this week she had the security of a roof over her head. Friday and Saturday night after wiping off her makeup, she'd left her face clean. Knowing Patrick and his family were waiting in the lobby for her tonight, she applied a touch of bronzer to her pale cheeks and a few swipes of mascara on her lashes.

The elaborate braids Fiona had done in her hair would have to stay, unless she wanted to take them out and deal with the frizz and gobs of hairspray. Last night she'd brushed her out and knotted it up in a messy bun. Not tonight though.

Making sure she had her area cleaned up, she dressed in her jeans and sweatshirt and zipped up her winter coat.

A crew much larger than she expected cheered for her as she rounded the corner.

"Oh, Jocelyn. You were wonderful. Your voice is beautiful." Mrs. Johnson enveloped her in a warm hug.

"Thank you."

"Dude. You rocked this place if that even makes sense. Those are some seriously powerful lungs you've got on you, girlfriend." Liberty hugged her as well.

April pried them apart. "She's my roommate. I should've been the first to tell her how fabulous she is." She turned to Jocelyn. "You were. You are. I'm now embarrassed you've heard me sing in the shower. There's no way I could ever compete with a voice like yours. And your acting was perfect as well. What a fun play."

"We're going to bring Gabe with us next time. He'd love it." Noel offered a hug as well.

"Beautiful," Mr. Johnson added with his hug. "No wonder my son is so enamored of you."

Heat crept up her neck, and she was thankful for the scarf covering how red and blotchy her skin must be.

"Dad. You guys are embarrassing her." Patrick came to her aid and stepped in front of her, giving her an awkward smile. "You were—" he cast a sideways glance at his sisters who were smirking with delight— "phenomenal." He handed her a small bouquet of flowers.

For some reason, his praise meant more to her than the others. Taking the flowers, she brought them to her nose and breathed in their fresh scent. No man had ever brought her flowers before.

"Aww. So cute," Liberty chirped in.

"Hunter and Maria wanted to come as well but they couldn't find a sitter. We're babysitting next weekend, so they can tag along with Noel and Ian," Mrs. Johnson said.

"I appreciate you all coming tonight. This means a lot to me." More than they could possibly know.

"We'd like to take you out for a late dinner, if you don't already have plans," Mr. Johnson said.

"I didn't know if you were going out with your crew." Patrick's gaze flicked over her shoulder where Sarah and other cast members were laughing.

She and Patrick stood elbow to elbow with their coats as barriers but she swore she could feel his warmth, and his nervousness.

She smiled warmly at his family. "I'd be honored to have dinner with all of you." Again. Again and again she'd love to sit at a table surrounded by this family that emanated warmth and love. "I should check on Cocoa first."

"I took him out for a run an hour before I left," April said. "And I filled his bowl with kibble and made sure he had fresh water and his chew toys. I'm sure he can handle another hour of having the place to himself."

Another thing she hadn't needed to worry about. "Thank you," she said from the bottom of her heart. They'd all accepted her into their lives without a question, without judgment, not that they knew how she'd been living. Patrick knew, and how he looked at her now was completely different from how he had at Thanksgiving.

His dark eyes were softer, the tight lines she'd noticed around his mouth were smoother.

"We made reservations at the Steak House. We'll get a head start and make sure the table's ready," Mrs. Johnson said, looping her arm through her husband's and giving her daughters a raised eyebrow.

They responded with grins.

"I'll catch a ride with Liberty," April said. "Don't be long, you two."

When they left, Patrick explained. "April rode here with me."

"Oh." She still held her flowers close to her chest. "Thank you for these."

Patrick tucked his hands in his coat pockets and nodded over his shoulder to where a florist had set up a shop. "I saw other people getting them and didn't know... I figured... I... I wanted you to have them."

In other words, it wasn't a romantic gesture, and he wanted her to know that.

It was bad enough his family thought there was something going on between them. She'd put him out of his misery by letting him know she didn't view the gesture as anything more than friendly.

"Yes. She has a nice gig here. Having her flowers in the lobby makes people think they have to buy them for their friends or family in the show, or for their dates. The producer let her set up for opening weekend."

She tucked the bouquet in the crook of her arm and searched through her purse for her keys. "I guess we should get going." Without looking to see if he followed her, she moved past him to the front doors.

Before she could reach for the handle, Patrick was there opening the door for her.

"Thank you."

He still hadn't said anything as he followed her to her car. When she opened it, he stood there like he had last time. "The restaurant is two miles—"

"I know where it is." She didn't mean to sound so biting. She closed her eyes and tucked her chin to her chest. "I'm sorry. You've been nothing but nice to me."

"Hey." He tipped her chin up with the back of his hand. "You've had a long day. A long weekend. If you're not up for going out, that's okay. I can see you home."

"That's not it at all."

"Then what is it?"

With a heavy sigh, she rolled her shoulders and feigned a smile. "Maybe I'm a little tired, but I have Monday and Tuesday off to recover. Besides, I love spending time with your family." *Especially you.*

Again, her cheeks warmed. It was so cold and dark out she didn't think he'd notice.

"My family can be exhausting." He pulled his ringing cell from his pocket and chuckled. "Liberty. I'm sure they all want to know if I kidnapped you."

Jocelyn grinned. "We shouldn't keep them waiting." She slid behind the wheel and warmed up her car. While she put on her gloves, she watched Patrick jog across the parking lot. When she pulled out, she kept an occasional eye on the headlights following her to the restaurant.

The car pulling up next to her was an unfamiliar Jeep. She'd never had an experience with a stalker or anything, but spending so many years in New York City trained her to always be alert. Keeping her engine running and her doors locked, she waited until she could make out the driver.

Patrick.

She turned off her car and stepped outside. "I didn't recognize the vehicle."

"Smart of you to stay in the car then. My off-duty wheels. I keep it parked at the station when I use the cruiser."

That made sense. "I wanted to be sure."

"You okay?" His sincerity caught her off guard, like he really wanted to know if she was. It wasn't the blanket "Hi. How are you?" greeting for when you didn't expect an honest reply. The sincerity in his dark eyes told her he really did care.

"I'll get my second wind once I sit down, I'm sure."

"My family won't give you a choice, but say the word and I'll come up with an excuse for us to leave." He took her gloved hand in his like it was an everyday occurrence, the norm between the two of them.

Again, he held the door open for her. "I can hear them." She laughed and followed the sound of Liberty's voice.

"It's about time. We were about to put an APB for you two," Liberty teased.

There weren't even any water glasses on the table, so she knew she and Patrick hadn't stayed too long talking. Even so, the smiles and laughter from the six of them around the table made it clear they were all poking fun.

Jocelyn only hoped it didn't make Patrick wary of spending time with her. She'd need to let him know she knew he was only being kind and that his gestures were out of manners and not a romantic interest.

He pulled out a chair for her and waited for her to take off her coat and sit before filling the spot next to her. Their waitress came over and asked for their orders.

Jocelyn scanned the menu for the cheapest item. She ordered a chicken salad and hot tea.

"Is that a singer thing? Does it warm or loosen your vocal cords or something?" April asked after they all placed their orders.

"Both, I suppose. Plus, it's so cold outside I can't imagine drinking ice water." Which was what the rest of them ordered, as well as two bottles of wine to share.

"So, tell us," Mrs. Johnson leaned forward with excitement, "where else have you sung? My church choir would love to have you join us."

"Mom. Your choir is full of eighty-year-old fuddy-duddies."

"Your mother is no fuddy-duddy."

"Nor am I eighty." She poked an elbow into her husband's side. "Liberty, when was the last time you went to church?"

"Not this again," she moaned. "I work a lot of Sundays, Mom. The big stories don't just happen from Monday through Friday between eight and five."

"I'm aware. You could come hear your mother sing in the choir from time to time. We can't compete with Jocelyn, but we hold our own. You all said you'd do your best to attend the Christmas concert in a few weeks."

"Mom's been trying to get the five of us to join her since we were born. Noel sang for a few years in high school. April tried her hand at it as well, but got booted out."

"I wasn't that bad."

"We didn't kick her out."

"Please, Mom. When I was fifteen, you all said I could play the tambourine. I knew it was to drown out my voice."

Jocelyn couldn't remember a time when she'd laughed so much. Maybe three nights ago at Thanksgiving, but tonight she was more carefree and less nervous about them learning about her being homeless and living out of her car.

"What are your plans for when the play is over? Do you have the next production lined up?" An innocent question, one Mrs. Johnson wouldn't have asked had she known the answer.

"I'm not exactly sure. I've been looking for auditions...in the south."

"Oh." They all glanced at Patrick, who'd been quiet.

The waitress came with their meals—a welcome distraction. It was quiet for a few minutes as they all dived into their food. Her stomach wasn't as empty as it had been an hour ago. Now the weight of guilt filled it.

Guilt from leading this nice family along like they'd be lifelong friends lodged in her throat. Her time in Maine was limited. In less than a month the show would end, and she'd be driving south.

"In the meantime," Noel piped up after a long silence, "if you're looking for something around here, our school district is always in need of substitutes. In fact, the music teacher at the middle school is pregnant and going on maternity leave in late January. Or sooner if her baby decides to make an early appearance. Anyway, as far as I know, they haven't found a long-term sub for her."

"I don't know anything about teaching."

"Which is why subbing is a perfect way to get your feet wet. You love animals, which are pretty much like mini humans anyway, and you were great with Gabe and the Georgia the other night. You have the disposition to be a teacher."

Teaching? She'd never given it a single thought. Besides, she didn't have a college degree. No way would a school hire her. She didn't want to admit she didn't have a degree while surrounded by an obviously well-educated family.

"You'd have to get fingerprinted. State law," Noel added. They all looked at Patrick who opened his mouth to speak and wisely closed it again. "I'm assuming the big guy wouldn't be sitting so close to you if you had a record."

"All our boyfriends were guilty until proven innocent. We didn't need Dad scaring them away when we had Mr. Macho here." April, on the other side of Patrick, patted his back.

"You guys are the ones giving her the third degree, not me."

What he most likely meant was he didn't have a clue if she had a record or not. Unless he looked her up. It was fine if he did. She was clean. The closest she ever got to breaking the law was when he tapped on her window and told her there was no overnight parking allowed.

The conversation switched to Noel and her pregnancy and somehow looped back to Jocelyn again.

"I'm serious about you helping with the gender-reveal party."

"My wife always gets her way." Ian kissed Noel's cheek. "The Johnson women are a strong-willed group."

"I wouldn't ask you to pay a dime for anything."

"Libs and I have it all planned. We'll take care of ordering the cake and balloons and the rest of the party, but we need you be the messenger," April said.

"Because I don't trust my sisters or my mother—"

"And to think I was going to make you my favorite daughter," Mrs. Johnson joked.

"—with the envelope," Noel continued. "Or peeking in the box of balloons. They'd find a way to cheat."

"No offense, sis." Liberty held up her wine glass in salute.

"The challenging part is finding a time when everyone is free."

"And even then, I never know when there will be a breaking story I'll have to cover. If I miss it, someone better Facetime me." Liberty lifted her wine glass and sipped.

"You know mine. Four days on, three days off," Patrick said.

"What is your schedule like, Jocelyn?"

"Mine?" She would've laughed if Noel hadn't been so serious. Jocelyn's schedule had been a whole lot of nothing. Except now for the play. "My weekends are really crazy, and since you work midweek, I don't know how I'd be able to help."

"I read the show times in the lobby. Sundays your first one will be two o'clock, right? What if we did a brunch reveal? Maybe around ten? What time do you have to be at the Playhouse?"

"Not until noon."

"Patrick, are you working next Sunday?"

"I'm free."

"Jocelyn? Can you make it work?"

"Three days ago, you didn't even know I existed. Are you sure you want me to have such an important role in your gender-reveal party?"

Noel leaned her head on her husband's shoulder. "It only took three days for me to fall in love with Ian."

"She's a slow learner." Ian draped his arm around Noel's shoulder. "It took me less than one."

"Enough." Liberty pushed back her chair. "I have to be in the studio bright and early tomorrow. Thanks for dinner, Mom and Dad." She hugged them both and then went around the table giving her siblings and brother-in-law a hug. "Don't be a stranger. Patrick can give you my cell. We'll do lunch." She hugged Jocelyn and then flitted away through the restaurant.

"We should go too." Noel laid her napkin on her plate. "School night. I'm sure Gabe is having a blast at his friend's house, but we promised we wouldn't be too late." She and Ian followed suit with a round of hugs. "Patrick. Give her my number as well."

April and Patrick both knew she didn't have a cell phone, but neither said anything. When the waitress brought the bill, Patrick took out his credit card and handed it to her. "You covered Thanksgiving, I've got tonight," he said to his parents.

"That's sweet of you, honey," his mother said.

"Show off," April teased as she hugged her brother. "Thanks for din. See ya at home, roomie." She kissed her parents on the cheeks and left.

"Let me pay my portion." Jocelyn unhooked her purse from the back of her chair and put it in her lap.

"No." He placed his hand over hers. "It's my treat."

"But you—"

"I want to. It was my idea for the family to celebrate your success together."

She glanced over at his parents who were putting on their coats. "Your sisters think—"

"It's not a big deal. We all take turns. Mostly my parents. Noel, and Hunter and Maria host meals at their homes, while I lean towards the takeout or dine-out options. April and Liberty end up contributing a lot to the home-cooked meals. Like Noel's gender-reveal party thing they've got coming up. Anyway, we're square."

So dinner once again wasn't of the romantic nature, a celebration of the success of the show was all. Jocelyn could live with that. Patrick signed when the waitress came back. He stood, offering his hand to help Jocelyn up, not that she needed it.

Manners. He inherited them from his father who had his hand in his wife's and was whispering something sweet in her ear. She could tell by the twinkle in Mrs. Johnson's eyes.

"I'm going to bring some of my girlfriends to your show soon," Patrick's mom said. "They'll love it, I know."

"I look forward to seeing you again."

When it was just the two of them, Patrick gestured with his hand for her to start out first. They thanked their waitress and braced themselves for the cold air. "I take it you're going to follow me home again, Officer?"

"It's just Patrick tonight." His gaze lingered with hers longer than it had before.

She wouldn't look into it, wishing it was something more. Avoiding his gaze, she opened her car door and gave him a wave with her fingers. "Thank you for dinner. Again. I'll see you around."

Before he had a chance to respond, she slipped behind the wheel and closed the door. The drive home took less than twenty minutes, not nearly enough time for her to get her thoughts together. Patrick looked especially nice tonight in his black button down and khakis. The dark shirt should have made his even darker features appear imposing, but it only brought out the depth in his eyes and emphasized his chiseled chin and cheeks. She parked at the duplex and headed to the door.

She was still thinking about his warm smile when a car door closed behind her. She started and turned to see Patrick crossing the patch of lawn between their front doors.

"Jocelyn." He stood on the bottom step, and with her two steps above him, they were still close enough for her to smell his aftershave. Clean and spicy.

Their eyes were now level. She'd never considered her five-foot six frame short, but next to Patrick she felt small. Feminine small, not like he loomed over her.

"Long time no see," she joked, hoping her nerves weren't evident in her voice.

"Tomorrow. Um..." he rubbed his hand across his face. "You said you didn't have to work?"

"I have two days off." This was it. He was going to tell her she needed to find a new place. That he didn't like the idea of her loafing around his sister's apartment while she worked all day.

"What are you doing tomorrow?"

"I, uh..." *Nothing.* Absolutely nothing, only she couldn't tell him that because he'd think she was a lazy mooch. "I need to send in my auditions to a few places." It was sort of a lie. That's what she wanted to do, but so far she hadn't found any plays that were casting nobodies with no formal vocal or theater training. Some lessons here and there were all she had. A natural talent her voice coaches had said. Still, that didn't look good on a résumé.

"Oh, okay." Patrick glanced away, licked his lips, then returned his intense gaze her way again. "If you'd like to do something, it's my day off. I could...show you around if you'd like."

First knight in shining armor, now tour guide. Once again Jocelyn told herself not to make a bigger deal of this than necessary.

"Know of any places that are dog friendly?"

"Not off the top of my head, but I know someone who does." That adorable grin was back, revealing a cute little dimple in his chin.

It should be illegal to have eyes as dark as his that still twinkled in the moonlight.

"I guess I'll see you tomorrow then."

"Tomorrow." He backed away, that grin still lighting up his face. "Tomorrow it is."

CHAPTER SIX

Patrick couldn't wipe his goofy smile off his face, even when his sister called him on it. "I could be scowling into the phone right now."

"You sound different," April said from the other end of the line. "I can hear it in your voice. Jocelyn's pretty tight-lipped when it comes to your relationship. You sure you two are a thing?"

"I told you a hundred times." He reached for the cream cheese in the fridge and set it by his bagel. "We're not in a relationship. We're friends. You and the rest of the family need to stop pressuring her. Us."

"Yeah. Sure. Right. Anywho, dog stuff. It's not as cold today as it was this weekend, so you could try the dog park in Portland. Maybe go for a walk around the cove? Hike a mountain? There are a bunch of coffee shops in Portland that allow dogs. Walk around the Old Port and then stop inside one to get warm. Share a cup of chocolate and stare into each other's eyes?"

"You're exhausting."

"And you love me for it. Look. Gotta go. My nine o'clock is here and he's a biter."

Patrick's phone went silent and he tossed it on the counter. A day outside in the fresh air would be nice. He didn't know much about Jocelyn other than her love for music and dogs. She'd mentioned going for long walks and wanting to cross-country ski when there was enough snow on the ground, so she had to have some sort of love for the outdoors.

Instead of rushing to call her like he really wanted, he sat down at the kitchen table with his coffee and bagel and scrolled through the daily news on his phone. Four bites later, he closed out of the news app

72

and dialed April's landline. She was notorious for forgetting to charge her phone and the family had insisted she have a landline for emergencies. Hopefully Jocelyn would answer it. She did.

"Still interested in a guided tour?"

"I'd love one."

There was an edge of excitement in her voice. Patrick told himself it didn't mean anything more than a cure for her boredom.

"Perfect. Dress warm. We'll be outside, if that's okay."

"After being inside the theater from nearly sunup to well past sundown, I can't wait to see the sun."

"Is thirty minutes too soon to pick you up?"

"I'll be ready."

"Perfect. I'll see you then. Unless I hit traffic." He cringed at his stupid joke. Thankfully it earned him a giggle from the other end of the line. Jocelyn's laughter was as pretty as her singing.

He busied himself by vacuuming and throwing a load of laundry in the wash. Twenty-eight minutes later, he laced up his boots and bundled up in his winter coat and hat.

Jocelyn opened her door seconds after he knocked, as if she was waiting for him by the door. "Hi."

His breath hitched. She shouldn't have that effect on him, especially covered from head to toe in winter gear. Only her face was uncovered. Her cheeks were rosy, her eyes dancing with delight.

"You look..." What? Beautiful? She did, she always did, but telling her so while bundled up might make him appear...obsessed. No, that was too strong a word. Interested. Well, he was. "Warm." It seemed to be the safest word.

"I'm wearing long johns under my jeans and three layers under my sweatshirt. If we don't leave soon, I'm going to sweat through all this."

She stepped out and closed the door behind her. Patrick looked down by her feet in confusion. "Did you want to bring Cocoa?"

"I didn't know where we were going and I hate to leave her in the car. Besides, I doubt you want dog hair in your Jeep."

"I planned the day with Cocoa in mind."

"You did?" Her coffee-colored eyes grew wide and still as if shocked. After a moment, she blinked rapidly and covered her mouth with her fingers.

"Is that okay?"

"It's more than okay. That was very sweet of you."

Sweet wasn't a word most used with him. He was too big, too surly, too grumpy, his sisters would argue. "Sure." He tucked his hands in his pockets and shrugged as if it was no big deal.

He waited outside while she went in for Cocoa.

She brought the dog out on a leash a minute later. "I can't tell you how much I appreciate this. How much it means to me that you included Cocoa in our day."

"I figured since you've been working so much, you'd want to be with her." It was true, mostly, and if it helped to convince her to spend the day with him, all the better. He opened the passenger side of his Jeep for the two of them.

"Would you rather she sit on my lap or in the backseat?"

"Wherever you'd like is fine with me."

"She's been used to riding shotgun, but when my sister was with me, she loved having the backseat to herself. She's small but loves to sprawl."

"I have a blanket in the back I can get for her."

While Jocelyn helped Cocoa into the backseat, Patrick got the blanket and placed in next to the dog. "Not sure what to do with it."

"Are you sure? I can get one of hers from inside."

"It's an emergency blanket so it's nothing fancy."

"You're very sweet."

That word again. It didn't exactly make him uncomfortable. Not itchy in a bad way. Unfamiliar. That was a better description.

When they were buckled in and Cocoa had her nose stuck to the backseat window, he pulled out of the driveway.

"Sorry I didn't think to warm up the Jeep before getting you."

"I never think to run out early and warm up my car. It wasn't something I had to do when living in the city, and lately..." Her words trailed off and she shrugged her shoulder.

"How long have you been..."

"Homeless?" she said with a laugh.

"I'm sorry. It's none of my business. I shouldn't have—"

"It's okay. I figured you had me checked out after busting me twice last week."

He cleared his throat and opened his mouth to deny it, then thought better and didn't respond.

They drove in silence for a while before she continued. "I haven't had a place of residence since July thirty-first."

"Four months is a long time to be without a roof over your head."

"It hasn't been that bad. At least, not until the nights got colder. This summer I lived in campgrounds. Cocoa loved socializing with the other dogs, and I loved my privacy. I have a tent, a sleeping bag, and some basic camping essentials in my car. It got us through fall. November's been the tricky month with nothing open in New England."

"Which is why you're heading south after the play finishes up?"

"Yeah."

That gave him only a month to get to know her. A month and then she'd be gone. "If I hadn't...if April hadn't asked you to room with her, you'd be sleeping in your car still, wouldn't you?"

"First, I know it was Cocoa who suggested to April that I room with her. And for that I will be forever thankful."

"And second?" He didn't want her to ignore his question. His concern for her safety and well-being was more than a police officer's need to know. Much more.

"I would never let Cocoa suffer. If it became too cold, I would have gotten us a motel room."

Which would eat up what little money she had. "I'm glad I was on duty on Thanksgiving and found you." She turned to him and he did all he could not to stare at her and soak up her innocent beauty.

"Me too."

The ride to Portland didn't take long. He pulled into a parking spot in the Back Cove lot and was surprised at how many cars were there. In the warmer months it was always busy. The three-mile path around the cove was a popular place for runners, walkers, and bike riders.

"Have you ever been here before?"

"Never," she said. "If you can believe it, I've never even driven to Portland."

"It's only twenty minutes north of Wilton Hills." Not that she lived in Wilton Hills. She lived nowhere. He kicked himself for being an idiot and got out of the car.

Jocelyn and Cocoa were already out by the time he reached their side. Cocoa's tail wagged in excitement, her little paws dancing in circles around their feet. "I think Cocoa approves."

They started on the path and Cocoa pulled at the leash. "She wants to run. Do you mind? She tires easily after a mile or so."

Running wasn't his favorite form of exercise. His boots weren't exactly going to help his speed, but he figured he already had an advantage with legs a heck of a lot longer than Jocelyn's. And about a million times longer than the little beagle's.

"Let's do it."

They set out at a slow jog, and then Jocelyn and Cocoa picked up speed. Patrick did all he could to keep up with them. Sweat beaded on his forehead, and he was tempted to take off his winter hat. The movement would have slowed him even more so he pumped his arms to maintain stride next to her.

His heart raced and his throat, dry from the cold air, burned. His legs were used to an intense workout in the gym deadlifting and squatting three hundred pounds. A ten-minute cardio run on the treadmill was his basic warm up before lifting, but even then he never pushed himself. It was supposed to be a warm-up after all.

Jocelyn must have heard his huffing and glanced at him over her left shoulder. "Do you run this trail often?"

If he had the energy, he would have laughed. "Not in a long time." Not since he was in his early twenties and even then, it had been warm and he had worn running shoes.

"It's beautiful here. The city skyline across the water makes it feel like a smaller version of Central Park. Not really, but quite different from Wilton Hills."

"Do you miss it? New York?" Puffs of air escaped his mouth as he huffed along next to her.

"I thought I would," she said easily as if the run caused no strain on her lungs. "I used to think Albany was too small and that I belonged in a big city like New York."

"You miss Albany?"

"There's nothing there for me either."

Cocoa went off the trail and sniffed around a tree. Thankful for the break, Patrick leaned over and rested his hands on his thighs as his heart rate slowed. When Cocoa had done her business and Jocelyn cleaned up after her with a plastic bag, he straightened.

"Are you okay?" She reached for him, but looked at the plastic bag of dog poo and retreated.

Patrick couldn't help but laugh. "I've always prided myself with how in shape I am. You and that little beagle of yours put me to shame."

He could tell she tried to hide her smirk. "We also don't have heavy boots on our feet," she pointed out.

"True." Nodding at the plastic bag, he said, "There's a receptacle up ahead for that. Too many people don't clean up after their pets."

"I noticed a water station for dogs a ways back. It looks like the town had pet owners in mind when they made the trail."

"Those didn't come until later. People and their pets are appreciative though."

"We can walk the rest of the way."

She was too gracious to point out his heavy breathing, although it had subsided some. "I don't want to hold you two back."

"I'm pretty sure that mile stretch did Cocoa in. When she stops to...sniff around, that usually means she's ready to cool down."

They continued around the cove until they came to the split-off. "It's about another mile back to the Jeep, or we can branch off to the left and head into the Old Port."

"I don't want to keep you. If you have other plans today—"

"To the Old Port it is." There were more people and a lot of traffic in the roads, but Cocoa did great staying by Jocelyn's side. When he spotted the coffee shop he'd found online earlier, he stopped. "Feel like warming up with a coffee or something?"

"I'll be up all night if I have another cup."

"Oh. Okay." He tried to hide the disappointment in his voice.

"I could go for a cup of tea or hot cocoa though."

Her response shouldn't have caused a stirring in his chest. It was silly but his heart had a mind...or rather, a beat of its own.

"It's dog friendly," he said as he held the door open.

"Are you sure? I don't see a sign."

"I looked it up this morning. There." He pointed at the tiny sign in the lower corner of the window.

"You looked it up?" They stood practically toe to toe in the doorway. He had a solid six inches on her and she had to crane her neck to look up at him. For a moment, he was lost in her eyes, in the slight blush across her cheeks.

Breaking the mood, he placed a hand on her lower back and guided her inside. "We're letting all the cold air in." They stood in line and read the chalkboard menu hanging behind the counter. "I don't know about you, but that sprint you made me do left me hungry. Would you like a pastry to go with your drink?"

"Sprint?" She giggled. "And here I thought you were the athletic type." As if surprised by her comment, she bit her lip as her cheeks darkened to an adorable rosy red.

"I thought I was too. I'm going to need some serious amounts of carbs if I have to keep up with you and that little pooch of yours all the way back to the Jeep."

"We'll take it slower. Besides," she looked down at Cocoa lying on the floor by her feet, "I'm pretty sure we're going to be carrying her back."

"Now that I can handle."

They placed their order and he paid while she found them a table. While he waited for the barista to make their drinks, he took a minute to check out the place. Trendy. Hipster he guessed, not that he knew exactly what that meant. The wide wood planks on the floor were worn in a rustic, distressed way, not in a condemned-farmhouse way.

Coffee paraphernalia and quotes decorated the forest green walls. Mugs, jams, teas, and other locally made goods for sale were on two shelves, and the glass cabinet next to the register held cupcakes, cookies, and pastries.

Jocelyn had picked out a cranberry-orange muffin while he chose a cinnamon roll. When their order was ready, he tucked the bag with the pastries under his arm and carried their hot chocolates where she sat toward the back. Cocoa had made herself comfortable on a mat designated for dogs.

"She looks passed out already."

"Fair warning, Cocoa snores. I never realized it until our first night camping."

"Maybe it's all the fresh air?" He set their drinks down before taking a seat across from her.

"Could be. I haven't noticed it the past couple nights. I know April's been wearing her out during the day, but she doesn't snore as loud when she's at the foot of my bed compared to when she's on the ground next to my sleeping bag or on my lap in the car." She ducked her head as if embarrassed by her last comment.

He reached out and squeezed her hand. "I'm glad you both have a soft bed to sleep in."

Those doe eyes lifted to his. "Me too." Her gaze didn't stay locked with his for too long. She looked away and moved her hand from his.

It was nice for a moment. Her fingers were still cold from outside, even with gloves on. They sipped their hot chocolate and talked over their pastries. He had no idea how much time had passed. All he knew was that he didn't want their time together to end.

He hadn't thought much past the walk and the coffee shop. Was it too presumptuous to ask her to spend the entire day with him? When she got up to use the ladies' room, he bought a dog biscuit and gave it to Cocoa.

"You'll need your energy too, little nugget. If your legs can't keep up with your Speedy Gonzales mom, I'll carry you, okay?" He rubbed behind her ears as she crunched on her biscuit.

"You're spoiling her," Jocelyn said from behind him.

"Busted." He stood and wiped his hands on his jeans. "Would you like to explore the Old Port or head on back?"

"What's there to do in the Old Port?"

"In nicer weather they have festivals, sidewalk sales, and concerts. In the winter the tree lighting, which they did on Friday. Not much on a Monday afternoon. A lot of the shops are decorated for Christmas."

"I loved looking at the Macy's Christmas displays. They're amazing."

"You're not going to see anything to that scale here. We're pretty low-key and simple in Maine."

It seemed no matter what he did she'd find comparisons to the big city. The spark in her eye and excitement in her voice picked up a notch whenever she talked about it. They'd talked about the Christmas trees earlier. The one in the center of town wouldn't impress her after seeing the ones in Rockefeller Center for so many years.

"I'd love to see Portland's tree."

"It's not that grand," he reminded her.

"It's bigger than any tree I've had in my apartments, I'm sure."

His heart tugged a little, and an ache grew inside his chest for all the childhood memories she'd missed out on. The tree was another reminder of how little she'd had growing up, and as an adult. Patrick felt ashamed of himself for having a pity party at her leaving when she deserved to find some happiness in her life.

"It's prettier at night, but we can take a walk down there." He hooked the leash to Cocoa's collar and held on to it as Jocelyn put on her coat and hat. When she reached for the leash, he stopped her. "I've got her."

They hadn't made it too far down the sidewalk when Jocelyn *ahh'd.* "I love how every lamp post is decorated with garland and bows. And the awnings on the storefronts are so quaint. It's like a picture out of a book. Or a scene from a movie. It's so pretty and clean."

"Clean?" He wouldn't go that far. Not like the center of Wilton Hills. But it was a lot harder to keep a city of seventy thousand clean than a small town of four thousand.

"No one can argue about the magic of New York City."

And here comes another comparison. Patrick kept his mouth shut not wanting to start an argument by defending Portland. If she didn't like one of the biggest cities in Maine, so be it. She obviously wasn't meant to live in this small state.

"There's so much culture and diversity," she said. "There's always something to do, always something going on." He couldn't say the same for Maine. "But this is...nice."

Nice. Yes, it was. To him, it was great. Perfect. Beautiful. Beaches, mountains, city—on the small end, but still a city—community. That's what Maine was. To each his own. If that wasn't what Jocelyn was looking for in a permanent residence, then they were never meant to be anyway.

Not that he was looking for the happily ever after.

"I feel safe here." Her arm brushed against his. They walked closer together where the sidewalk was more crowded. "Portland is this fantastic balance of culture and hominess. I can see why you love it here. New York City is much prettier at night when you can't see the filth, the poverty, the decay. I like that Portland doesn't need the cover of darkness to be beautiful. I bet it's stunning though at night."

Feeling more relaxed with the direction of her chatter, he chimed in. "It is. The city lights reflecting off the water are pretty spectacular as well."

"Maybe we can come back? I'll treat you to a cocoa?" At the sound of her name, Cocoa's ears flicked and she twisted her head around.

"I'd like that." He took a risk and slipped his free hand in hers. Even with the barrier of their gloves, he liked being more connected to her. "So, you have an obsession with hot cocoa. Is that why you named her that?"

Jocelyn laughed, again the sound tickled his core. "My sweet tooth isn't *that* bad. She was three years old when Kimmy and I got her from the shelter and didn't want to confuse her by changing her name."

They walked up and down the sidewalks and he couldn't help the way his heart tugged every time she got excited at a store's window display.

"Oh, look at the beautiful nutcrackers. Kimmy and I used to collect figurines when we were younger. Our favorite was the Sugarplum Fairies. They're the only piece of our childhood I still have."

He watched her as she fixated on one of the glass fairies. The sun shining through the window sent prisms of light spraying from all around it as if it was real.

"Want to go inside? I can stay out here with Cocoa."

She slipped her hand free from his and tucked them in her pockets. "No. It's okay." She turned her back to the store, a sad smile tugging her lips downward. "It's not like I can afford—" She shook her head as if knocking away the words. A new smile, forced, etched her lips. "It's called window shopping for a reason."

When she picked up her speed down the sidewalk, he contemplated asking her to tell him more about her childhood, her teenage years. Her *now*. Instead, he tugged gently on Cocoa's leash, and when she didn't budge, he scooped her up in his arms and jogged to catch up with Jocelyn.

"Sorry," she said when he brushed up next to her. "I guess I... sometimes I get lost in my thoughts and—" she adjusted her knit hat, pulling it down farther over her ears "—well, we should probably head back to the car. Cocoa's spent."

"I don't mind carrying her if you want to walk around some more."

"No. It's okay." They turned around and headed back down the sidewalk in silence. Something shifted in the air around them.

The light in Jocelyn's eyes dimmed, and Patrick didn't know the right thing to say. Gloss over it and make a joke? He wasn't an especially funny guy. His sisters inherited that gene from their father. Maybe ask what was wrong? He had no right to pry into her life any more than he already had.

It was obvious being in Portland brought back memories of New York, the place she wished she was. A place with more opportunities for her career. Settling down in a humble town with a small-town cop would not satisfy a beautiful, talented woman like Jocelyn.

Summoning up the inner strength of a powerlifter, he made idle conversation about her play, his sisters, and the upcoming snowstorm the forecasters were predicting for Thursday. When they reached his Jeep, they waited for it to warm up before driving home in silence.

"Thanks for the outing. I had a nice time," she said after she let Cocoa out, who ran around the front yard as if she hadn't been home in ages.

Nice shouldn't have sounded so boring, but he supposed that's what he was. What Maine was to her. Just passing through on her way to bigger and better things.

"Sure. Anytime." Afraid if he walked her to the door, he'd be tempted to do something stupid like kiss her, he instead waited in the walkway between their two driveways until she was safely inside.

Closing the door to his apartment, he glanced around his living room and felt alone. Confused. And possibly in love with a woman who was so perfectly right for him. Too bad he was so perfectly not right for her.

CHAPTER SEVEN

Jocelyn didn't know what she did or said to upset Patrick, but ever since they left the dog-friendly coffee shop, he'd seemed utterly miserable. He was a hard one to figure out. If she acted too sunshiny and excited about their simple day, he'd think she was looking into the day as something more than a friendly gesture.

She'd been on plenty of dates. Every man who'd treated her to dinner wanted at least a kiss at the end of the night. And taking her to meet his family? Yeah, those men wanted something in return, which she wasn't about to do.

Yet Patrick had asked for nothing and made no advances on her. He only briefly held her hand. Once or twice he placed his hand on hers or on her lower back, but those gestures were out of politeness and not romantic interest.

She thought she did a good job of distancing herself, so he wouldn't know she was indeed interested in him as more than a friend. When she found herself getting too caught up in the excitement of a story, she'd noticed how more withdrawn Patrick became. Not that he wasn't interested in her story, but that he wasn't interested in *her*.

The awkward conversation about weather was a sure sign he wanted their not-quite-a-date to end. A good deed done by a nice man, that was all the past week was. She'd move forward, do her job, and then head south for the winter and hopefully back to New York in the spring.

Since Cocoa was wiped and already curled up in the dog bed April had brought home yesterday, Jocelyn logged into the computer to hunt for jobs. April had been more than generous, giving her the password, so she could research and send her résumé and portfolio to theaters along the East Coast.

An hour later and no new leads, she turned off the computer and went upstairs to take a shower. The day dragged on, the silence from inside and from next door making her feel more alone than when she lived at the campground last summer.

Having a taste of family and a glimpse of what it could be like to be with a man like Patrick made it even harder to go back to her life on the road. Alone.

The rest of the week dragged as well. The only highlight was when she went out to her car after an evening storm had dropped eight inches of snow, it was all cleaned off and the driveway plowed.

She'd called April when she got to work thanking her, but April replied it was Patrick who performed the good deed.

Patrick. The man who made her heart flutter and who had ignored her since they returned from their pleasant afternoon in Portland five days ago. She hadn't had a lot of time to wallow in her misery. When she wasn't at the Playhouse, she was running errands for Noel and Ian's gender-reveal party on Sunday morning.

Noel had stopped by with the sealed envelope with the gender yesterday and a list of things to buy, as well as cash to cover it all. Jocelyn couldn't help but over-analyze why she'd given her cash instead of a check.

She still had her bank account and was thankful for online banking. Not too many banks had branches all across the country, and she didn't know where she'd end up.

With the party supplies loaded in the back of her car, she looked forward to a night on stage where she didn't have the luxury of thinking about dark, brooding eyes that warmed her insides and confused her head.

Tomorrow morning would come soon enough and she'd have to face him again. The Johnsons and Ramos families would be in for a huge surprise at the party, which would be the perfect distraction from Patrick.

Thankfully her morning would be rushed, and she would help set up and then sneak out when the party really got started. The less time she had with Patrick the better. It was getting harder and harder to hide her feelings for him, and seeing him be the perfect brother, son, and uncle to those adorable kids would only seal the deal on her heart.

Not even this year's Academy Award winner could pretend she wasn't falling for a man like Patrick Johnson. It would be one heck of a show she'd have to put on, and Jocelyn wasn't sure if she was up to the challenge.

PATRICK REFUSED TO believe his phone alarm was telling the truth when it buzzed on the pillow next to his head. Exhausted after working four twelves in a row, the last being a graveyard shift, he felt around blindly for his phone and turned it off. Brent was down with the flu, and Patrick normally didn't mind picking up the extra shifts. If it wasn't for Noel and Ian's gender-reveal party in forty-five minutes, he'd have slept the day away.

If it was summer, the sun would have already been up by the time he got home this morning. Four hours sleep would have to suffice.

Rolling out of bed, he finally worked his eyes open and rubbed them on his way to the bathroom. He was excited for his sister and brother-in-law. He didn't know why they wanted to do this big gender-reveal thing. Boy or girl, he didn't care. He'd love his niece or nephew just the same.

Knowing his support was important to them, he quickly showered, shaved, and got dressed. While he waited for his coffee to brew, a car started outside. Not wanting to appear stalkerish, he went to the front window and peeked around the shade.

April. Jocelyn's car was already gone. It was better that way or he'd find himself offering her a ride, which was dumb because he already knew she had to leave the party to go to the Playhouse.

At least there'd be plenty of people at his sister's to distance him from Jocelyn. The last thing he wanted to do was make a fool of himself. More than he already had.

Returning to the kitchen, he poured his coffee into a travel mug and downed half of it before he reached his Jeep. His sisters were always amazed at how he could guzzle piping hot coffee. Never knowing when he'd get a call, he'd learned early on in his career to fuel up on caffeine quickly because his next opportunity for a shot of java might not come until the end of his shift.

His sister and Ian were still living in her old house close to their parents while they waited for their new house to be built in town. Their incomes were limited and they'd settled on a small three-bedroom cape that would be perfect for their growing family. It had a huge backyard with plenty of room for children to play and was close to the school.

Nice and cozy. Perfect for Noel. With his crazy schedule and inability to hold a steady relationship, the duplex-style apartment was perfect for him.

At the house, he parked behind Jocelyn's car, that unfamiliar and unwanted tugging in his chest happened again. His legs reached the front porch as if on a will of their own. As soon as he pressed the bell, Gabe opened the front door.

"Uncle Paddy! It's almost time to find out if I'm going to be a big brother or—" he scrunched his face as he realized his error— "if I'm going to have a little brother or a little sister."

"That munchkin in your mom's belly is pretty lucky to have you as a big brother. What are your bets on pink or blue balloons?"

"Blue. I don't like pink."

Patrick ruffled Gabe's hair. "Real men like pink and any other color."

"How come you never wear pink?"

Busted. "I don't have a bunch of colors in my wardrobe." He paused to think. "No orange, purple, yellow, red. I guess I'm pretty boring."

"You have a Red Sox shirt. Remember we got matching ones on Christmas?"

"You're right. I guess I do have a red shirt." It was really sweet. Gabe had wanted to fit in with the guys, so he'd asked Ian to get them all matching shirts.

"Honey, we're so glad you could make it. April told us about your extra shift." His mom gave him a warm hug, then his father and sisters followed suit.

"We won't keep you since we know you probably want to get back to bed." Noel kissed his cheek. "Thank you for coming. It means a lot to us."

"I wouldn't miss it for the world." He dropped his gaze to her belly. "Don't take this the wrong way, but you've gotten bigger since last week. How many pies did you bring home?"

"Brat." Laughing, she swatted his arm.

Now that his family had given their hugs and backed off a bit, he had a moment to take in the bounty in the kitchen. A punch bowl with no cups yet, five quiches, two casseroles of his mother's famous hash browns, fruit salad, and a plate of donuts took up the counter space from end to end.

There weren't any decorations out yet, but a box labeled "Ramos Baby" sat in the middle of the table. He was lying to himself pretending to be more curious about the food and decor than where Jocelyn was.

The door to the garage opened and closed and there she was, beautiful with her hair down and flowing across her shoulders. She wore a dark purple dress that made her appear classy and sophisticated, which she was. Hanging from her hands were two bags filled to the brim.

"Hi." His voice croaked.

"Hi." She shot him a nervous smile, her gaze assessing, like she couldn't figure him out.

Remembering his manners, he stepped toward her and reached for the bags. "Let me help."

His hands curled around hers before she released the straps and they'd made the exchange. They stood facing each other in awkward silence, even with the chaos of laughter and loud chatter happening all around them. It was like they were alone in the world. Alone in the narrow hallway, yes.

She hesitated, a shy smile making something in his chest twang. "Thank you."

"Sure." He snapped to attention. "Where should I put these?" Whatever was in the bags was covered with newspaper.

"Somewhere safe where prying eyes and hands won't get to it."

"Ah. Pink or blue?" He lifted one of the bags closer and pretended to peek.

"Hey! No cheating."

His teasing worked. She now wore a grin on her lips, which he matched with a mischievous smile of his own. "How much would it take to get it out of you? Boy or girl?"

"I can't be bought." She folded her arms across her chest and cocked her hip to the side. "What's your guess? I bet you're wrong though."

"Wow. Such faith in me." He chuckled, not at all offended.

"Hey, you two." Noel had spotted them in the hall. Patrick hid the bags behind his back when she leaned in to peek. "I don't think I can wait any longer. The suspense and surprise of it all is killing me."

Patrick glanced from one to the other, curious about the secret smile Noel and Jocelyn shared.

"If I can trust you and Patrick to not peek in the bags," Jocelyn said, "I'll get the balloons."

"Need any help?"

"I've got it." She slipped out into the garage and was back before he had time to tuck the bags under the kitchen island.

Without asking, he took the box from her, and once again their fingers mingled before she stepped back. A faint blush stained her cheeks.

"It's light," he teased, shaking the box, hoping to alleviate some of the tension between them.

"It's filled with air," she stated the obvious.

"Where do you want this?"

"The big show is happening in the living room." She brushed past him and he followed her joining the crowd.

"It's about time," April said in dramatic fashion. "You two sneaked away for so long we didn't know if you took off with all the pink decorations."

"Blue. Noel's carrying a boy. I mean, it's obvious." Liberty pointed to her belly. "Maria's baby bump was practically up to her neck. This one's dragging south."

"You just wait." Maria draped an arm across Noel's shoulders. "We'll see how your little bambino decides to hang out and push around your organs."

"I do think she's carrying low." Their mother tapped her finger to her lips. "My guess is a boy as well."

Noel grinned and reached for her husband's hand. Ian wore a goofy smirk too.

"Alex? What's your guess?" Ian rubbed Noel's belly.

"One thing I've learned in my thirty years of marriage—"

"Thirty-seven," Noel's mom corrected.

"Thirty-seven years of marriage," her dad continued, "is that your mother is always right."

"Excuse me? May birthday here." April pointed to herself. "Patrick? What's your guess? Hunter and Maria already gave us theirs before you got here."

"I say girl and Maria says boy," Hunter said, drawing his wife to his side. Georgia played with Cocoa on the floor next to them.

Everyone was paired off. Liberty and April nestled on the couch together. Gabe made a threesome with his parents. And then there was Jocelyn standing in the archway between the kitchen and living room.

They all waited for his guess. Patrick glanced around the room, full of smiles and excitement, and it wasn't even like the baby was coming for another five months. This is what his family did. Supported each other, loved each other, celebrated each other. Being part of such a solid family unit was something he'd taken for granted over the years.

It wasn't until he met Jocelyn that he'd taken the time to be grateful for all he had.

He tried to meet Jocelyn's gaze but she tipped her chin down, staring at her hands folded in front of her.

"What do you think, Jocelyn?" he said.

She lifted her head, her brows furrowed in confusion. "I already know so I can't exactly guess."

The room erupted in laughter and for a moment he felt like a fool. That's what she did to him. Not make him foolish, but made him forget what was going on around him. Patrick wasn't sure if that was a good or bad thing. If he was on the job, very bad.

In front of his family? Well, by the sound of their laughter, it could be good.

"He's a sore loser. Always cheating to win. Nice one trying to get Jocelyn to spill the beans. Not going to happen. We trusted her and she came through." Noel gave her a one-armed hug with her free hand.

"I wasn't trying to cheat." He never did. He questioned the rules. A lot. Questioned his brother and sisters whenever they were winning at cards, which wasn't often. "I'm going to say a girl. I can picture Noel surrounded in pink babies and nerf guns." He winked at Gabe

"Babies, huh?" Again, the cheeky smile from his sister.

"Sure. I can't imagine you two will stop at this one."

"Well, I think we waited long enough. You ready?" Noel looked up at Ian, and he leaned down and kissed her.

"Let's do this," Noel said.

"Wait. I'm not ready." Liberty took out her phone to video the moment. April joined her. "Okay. Go."

Noel and Ian pulled back the tape and lifted the flaps of the box. Out came a blue balloon.

"A boy! I knew it!" his father said.

Then a pink balloon floated in the air next to the blue one. They all gasped, and Patrick shot a look at Jocelyn who bit her lip as if fighting back a smile.

Noel and Ian were grinning ear to ear as well while Gabe and Georgia chased the strings on the balloons.

"Wait a minute. I'm confused. Which is it? Did you tell to her read the envelope first and to put the pink or blue balloon in depending on the gender?" Hunter asked Jocelyn.

"She's not an idiot, dear brother, but I think you are." Liberty got up and smacked him on the back of the head.

"I'm confused as well," his father said.

"Surprise!" Noel lifted her hands in the air. "We're having twins!"

A collective gasp followed by loud exclamations of excitement scared Georgia, who started crying. Hunter scooped her up and gave her a balloon.

"Twins?" Patrick's mother screeched, pulling Noel into a hug. "Did you know?"

"We found out a few weeks ago, but didn't know the genders. If it was only one, I would've let Ian talk me into keeping it a surprise until I delivered. But with twins, I'd rather know so we can do as much planning ahead as possible."

"I can't believe you're having twins. And one of each. I'm so excited." April did a quick dance in the middle of the living room and hugged Noel.

In typical Johnson family, they all talked at once, and there were more hugs. Patrick searched the room for Jocelyn. She'd disappeared. He found her in the kitchen unpacking the boxes. She opened a package and took out a pink tablecloth.

"Can I help?"

"Um. Sure. There's a blue one in the bag. The table is so big we needed two anyway, so I got one of each." She unfolded the pink one and spread it across the table.

He followed suit with the blue. She set pink and blue cups, plates, and plasticware on the table. Together they hurried to arrange the punch bowl and the food dishes. Not long after Jocelyn placed the last bowl on the table, his father and brother joined them in the dining area.

"It's so loud in here already with excitement I can't even imagine what it'll sound like with two more babies." Hunter poured himself a glass of punch and guzzled it.

Patrick draped his arm across his brother's shoulders. "Just think. It could be you and Maria with twins next time."

"Your mother always wanted twins. You were such a beast in her womb she swore there were two of you in there." His father poked him in the chest.

"I don't think you could have handled two of me. Noel being pregnant with twins must be God's way of punishing her for being the perfect child."

"Hey, I heard that." Noel entered and pulled at his earlobe like she used to do when they were little. "And twins are *not* a punishment. They're double the blessing."

"That's right." Their mother sported a disappointing frown on her lips.

"I was only kidding." Patrick dropped his arm from Hunter's shoulders and hugged his sister.

"Must be the pregnancy hormones. Maria was extra testy when she was pregnant too."

Noel shrugged off Patrick's arms and punched Hunter in the chest. "I am *not* testy."

Patrick couldn't help the chuckle that escaped his throat. He much preferred the wrath of the Johnson women on Hunter than himself.

"Don't think I didn't hear that. I hope you find the living room sofa comfy because that's where you'll be sleeping if you keep that up," Maria warned, planting both hands on her hips.

When Patrick coughed out another laugh, he became the recipient of raised eyebrows. Quickly he tamped it down and plastered on his best smile. "You ladies look lovely today. Can I offer you some punch?" Without waiting for a reply he filled two pink cups and two blue cups, handing them to his sisters, sister-in-law, and mother. He picked up another and filled it, turning to offer it to Jocelyn.

The crowd had filled the kitchen and dining area, but he didn't see her anywhere. With everyone distracted by the food table, he carried the cup into the living room.

No Jocelyn there either. Movement out the front window caught his eye causing him to nearly spill the drink.

Not bothering with a coat or shoes, he ran outside and down the steps, ignoring the cold and wetness from yesterday's snowfall on his stocking feet.

"Jocelyn," he called after her. She was nearly to the end of the driveway before she turned. He jogged to her. "You're leaving."

"Yes. I don't... I... need to get to work."

"I thought April said you didn't have to be there until noon?"

"Sure." She toyed with the zipper on her coat. "But I wanted to go over my lines again. It takes a while to get into hair and makeup, and I don't like being rushed."

He could call her on her lie, but his manners wouldn't allow him to. Instead, he held out the cup for her. "I brought you punch." His cheesy line brought a faint smile to her lips.

"Thank you." She took it but didn't drink.

They ran out of conversation, their gazes locked in some kind of invisible heated battle, and Patrick wondered what it was about her that rattled his cage.

"You're leaving because you think you don't belong." She avoided his stare and took a sip of the punch. "Noel wouldn't have included you if she didn't want you here. Heck, you were the first to know about the twins. And their gender. If anything, she and Ian will be offended if you leave."

His mother would smack him for being rude to her, but he didn't want her to leave. For selfish reasons mostly, but also because he knew she needed friends, and because she was too selfless to ask for anything for herself.

Even though she was moving in a few weeks and he wanted to protect his heart, he wanted what was best for her, and that included time with his sisters. With her friends.

"Will you come back inside?" She blinked back whatever words were on her lips and didn't reply. "Please. It would mean the world to my family."

Cocoa barked at a squirrel and pulled at her leash. "I guess she's not ready to leave either. I suppose we can stick around a little while longer."

Either. Meaning Jocelyn really didn't want to leave. Patrick couldn't help the curve of his lips, as if he'd just won a competitive game of touch football with the guys.

They walked side-by-side back up the driveway. "Bringing you back will win me some serious brownie points. I sort of dug myself into a hole by implying twins are a curse for Noel being so perfect in her childhood. Hunter did me a solid by one-upping my stupid comments, though so I may be in the clear. Still, I don't think I'll be excommunicated from the family now."

"I highly doubt my presence is enough to resurrect you from the curse your sister must have hexed you with." She laughed and it did something funky to his insides.

Last week he'd told himself he couldn't fall for her. Not only was he not good enough for her—nor was Maine—but she wouldn't even be around to ring in the new year. He'd had his share of girlfriends in the past. No one serious or long-term. They didn't like his inconsistent hours and his dedication to his family.

During the few weekends he had off there was often some sort of family event. A holiday, birthday, anniversary, or impromptu get-together. It took one backyard barbecue for him to learn Natalie didn't like kids. That ended their six-month relationship. There were others in the years since Natalie, but he'd learned from that experience and had never brought a woman to another family function.

Not that he'd *brought* Jocelyn to his family.

Only he had. One week ago for Thanksgiving. Had it only been one week since Jocelyn walked into his life?

"There you are." Liberty greeted them at the door. "Noel's going to eat all the buffalo chicken dip if you don't get in here." She tugged at Jocelyn's coat sleeve pulling her into the house.

"Should I have made a bigger batch?"

"You'd think a Crockpot full should be enough, but you've met our family. We like to eat." Liberty took Jocelyn's coat and handed it to Patrick as if he were a butler, and God bless her for not asking why Jocelyn was wearing a coat.

He forced himself not to bring the coat to his nose and breathe in the strawberry and floral scent Jocelyn carried. Crouching to Cocoa's level, he unhooked her collar and rubbed behind her ears. "I'm sure plenty of food will get dropped in there. Have at it, girl."

She took off in a hurry, Liberty and Jocelyn right behind.

He hung up her coat in the closet. When he closed the door, Noel came down the stairs with a worried expression on her face.

"You okay?" Patrick placed his hands on her shoulders and looked down at her belly. "The babies? Is something wrong?"

"No." Noel folded her hands across her belly. "It's not me. I'm fine. I heard from one of the teachers. Carrie, the music teacher at the middle school who is pregnant, was put on bed rest. Her blood pressure is through the roof and she still has eight weeks until her due date."

"Will she be okay?" Patrick didn't know much about all the pregnancy stuff. He remembered some of the buzzwords from when Maria was pregnant but mostly he tuned out when his brother would talk about centimeters, varicose veins, Lamaze, and breastfeeding.

"Sandy thinks so. There's a bit of bright news in all of this though."

"What's that?"

"Well, Sandy called because she remembered me talking about a friend of mine who had a music background and was looking for a job."

"Jocelyn?"

"I know it's earlier than expected, but do you think she'd be interested in substituting during the week? Do you think it would be too much?"

It would be a lot, working seven days a week during the craziest month of the year. But it would also keep Jocelyn in Maine a little longer. If the music teacher didn't deliver for another eight weeks and she took the standard six-week maternity leave, that would keep Jocelyn around for another three months. Maybe longer.

His heart sped up as he thought about seeing more of her.

"There's only one way to find out."

CHAPTER EIGHT

Jocelyn tossed and turned for over an hour reminiscing about her day. She'd known it would be busy with the party and then her performances. But then when Noel told her about the opportunity for a long-term substitute position at the middle school, well, things got more real.

There wasn't anything she could do about it today but that didn't stop her mind from racing. Tomorrow she'd fill out the application, upload her résumé, and go through whatever other hoops the school department needed from her.

The pay wasn't great but it beat no pay at all. And the best news, it meant stability for a few more months. That was, of course, if she even got the job. Noel seemed to think she was a shoo-in since their area had a shortage of teachers and substitutes. Granted, that was due to the low pay, but still, it was more money than she was making now.

What did she know about kids? And teaching? Doubt clouded her thoughts again as she tucked a pillow between her knees and snuggled another to her chest.

She pictured Patrick's sensitive eyes staring back at her when she told him she'd be staying in Wilton Hills for a bit longer. He'd be curious, surprised, and then...what? She had moments when she believed he had an honest interest in her, but other times he grew distant, almost pushing her away.

It had been almost a week since he took her to Portland, and they'd walked around Back Cove. The fact that he'd looked up dog-friendly places ahead of time warmed her soul and made her believe, if only for a minute, that he was truly interested in her.

Their afternoon had been picture perfect until they were strolling through the town and his entire demeanor changed. Jocelyn sighed and tried to remember what they were talking about.

The pretty shops. The decorations. New York. At one point he'd mentioned bringing her back at night when everything was lit up. Or was that her asking to come back?

Either way, she did want to see Portland at night. Being bold and assertive, she'd ask him tomorrow if he'd join her. If he turned her down, she'd take the hint and would drop the wild fantasies she had about building a relationship with him.

If he took her up on the offer...her heart raced and she could feel her neck and face warming with the thought of being with him again. It wasn't love. Couldn't be love. She enjoyed his company and loved his family was all.

With the comfort of her pillows and thoughts, she finally fell asleep.

DOG BREATH AND WET tongue woke her in the morning. "You stink, baby girl." Jocelyn pulled back the covers and patted the space next to her. "Come snuggle with your mama."

Cocoa padded around in a circle stepping on her legs before settling next to her. She nudged Jocelyn with her nose and gave another swipe of her tongue. A second later she was up on all fours taking the covers with her.

"Let me guess. You want me to get up from this warm bed to go play outside with you in the freezing cold." The weather forecast had predicted a few inches of snow during the nightfall. Nothing major but enough to make the morning commute slick. Not something she had to worry about. Yet.

Remembering all she had to do today to apply for the job, she climbed out of bed, Cocoa at her heels, and took care of business in the bathroom. When she returned to her room, she tugged on her thick, fuzzy lined socks and sweatshirt. Grabbing a scrunchie from her nightstand, she pulled her hair back into a messy bun and made her way down the stairs.

"Sorry if she woke you," April said, already dressed for work and coffee in hand. "I fed her and let her out, but she was insistent on going upstairs. I had hoped it was to snuggle."

"Not this one." Jocelyn rubbed Cocoa behind the ears. "She likes to snuggle during the day, or when I'm trying to do something."

"Kind of like how a baby likes to be rocked to sleep."

"I guess."

"Speaking of, great job on the party yesterday. I can't believe you kept the twin secret. Noel's going to have her hands full."

"At least she has Ian and Gabe. They seem to dote on her. They'll be wonderful."

"That they will." April picked up her phone. "Shoot. I'm running late. Got any plans for your day off?" she asked as she put on her coat and hat.

"Just getting everything together to apply for the job."

"I hope you get it." She screwed on the cap to her coffee mug. "The middle school principal's Dalmatian is a patient of mine. I'll be sure to put in a good word."

"I appreciate it."

When she was alone, she sat at the computer and pulled up the job listing. Her letters of recommendation would come from the producer and director at the Playhouse. When she got to the part where she needed to list personal recommendations, she wrote down April's and Patrick's names.

Cocoa stirred and scurried to the front door, barking at it. A moment later an engine started outside, not a car. It sounded more like a snowblower. Saving her progress, she got up and peeked out the window.

Covered head to toe in winter gear, Patrick pushed the snowblower down the driveway. Cocoa yipped again and jumped up at the door.

"Easy girl." She pulled Cocoa away. "No scratching the door. If I let you out you need to stay out of Patrick's way, okay?"

The pup wagged her tail in excitement.

Jocelyn opened the front door and called out to Patrick to warn him Cocoa was coming, but with his back facing her and the loud *purr* of the snowblower, she doubted he could hear. She stepped out onto the front step—already shoveled, most likely thanks to Patrick—and watched as Cocoa ran through the freshly fallen snow.

She chased her own tail and leaped through the banks lining the walkway before running in front of the snowblower.

"Cocoa, no!" she yelled, worried she'd get run over.

Patrick stopped, turned off the blower and got down on his knees with Cocoa. "Hey, girl. You scared me."

Oblivious to her possible near-death experience, she wagged her tail and leaped up at him. Patrick laughed, the sound reverberating through the air and sending tingles through Jocelyn's body. He looked up and over his shoulder at her.

"Hi." He gave Cocoa one more pat before getting up and walking over to her. "You're really not dressed to be outside."

She looked down at her clothes—pajamas—and gasped. "Cocoa wanted to go outside and I... well, I'm sorry. I didn't mean for her to bother you."

"She's no bother at all." They both watched as she ran around making zigzags across the front yard.

"I'll keep an eye on her and make sure she stays out of your way."

Patrick returned his gaze to her. "You might want to put on a coat and hat first." He pointed to her feet. "And some boots."

"Yeah." She bit her lip and crossed her feet. "It is a little cold out here."

"I'll watch Cocoa while you get layered up."

She opened her mouth to protest, to tell him she'd bring Cocoa inside, but this was exactly the opportunity she was looking for. She let herself back inside.

It didn't take her long to lace up her boots and put on her coat, gloves, and hat. For a brief moment she contemplated looking in the mirror and adding a dab of make-up. Whether or not she was wearing mascara wasn't going to make Patrick like her or not. And if it did, then he wasn't right for her anyway.

She found them toward the side of the duplex in a game of chase the snowball.

"Your arm will tire of this game before she will." Jocelyn made a snowball and chucked one in the air. It didn't go nearly as far as Patrick had been throwing his.

His next throw wasn't as far, bringing Cocoa in closer to them. A pity throw, she figured. She packed another ball of snow and hurled it through the air. This time Cocoa caught it with her mouth, and the snow covered her muzzle.

"Good shot." Patrick chuckled.

"She has an easier time catching them when they're not missiles thrown at warp speed."

"Will she fetch a stick?" He broke a thin branch from a nearby oak tree and hurled it through the air. It sank into the snow and disappeared from site. Cocoa came up with it in a matter of seconds. "I guess so."

They played for a while until Cocoa shook off her coat and ran up the steps. "Looks like you tuckered her out. Thank you."

"She was a great distraction to my morning chores."

The driveway only had one clean swipe from the snowblower. There wasn't enough snow to cause much difficulty getting out, but enough to cause a mess. "Do you need a hand?"

"I'm good, thank you though. The walkway and steps are done. The driveway won't take too long."

Mustering up her courage, she looked him square in the eye and asked, "I was thinking of going into Portland tonight to check out the tree and the lights. Would you like to join me?"

Patrick wiped the snow from the front of his coat and looked over his shoulder toward the driveway. "I have to work."

"Oh. Okay." Her heart sank. He didn't sound disappointed. If anything, relieved he had an out not to spend time with her. "I'll let you get back to snowblowing."

She turned and jogged up the steps and inside, closing the door firmly behind her. She didn't know why she'd fled so quickly. Her eyes watered and a lone tear escaped, tracing a path down her cheek.

That was why. She didn't want him to see how disappointed she was with his rejection. She didn't blame him, really. What did she have to offer someone as...perfect as Patrick Johnson?

He was the type to want stability, family. She had neither. Once again, she mistook his kindness for genuine attraction. Refusing to make a fool of herself again, she made a promise to herself to stay far away from him. They were neighbors. He was her roommate's brother. Other than that, they had no connection.

Kicking herself for being a romantic fool, she sat behind April's laptop and continued her job search.

UNFORTUNATELY, THE excitement of the holidays usually brought more domestic dispute calls to the station. However, this week the calls were few and far between. Patrick should have been grateful. Instead the week dragged.

It could have also been because of the guilt eating away at his gut from his rudeness to Jocelyn a few days ago. He more than wanted to go with her to see the tree in downtown Portland all lit up. He wanted to watch her eyes shine with excitement again as she pointed out the holiday decor.

But he didn't know if he could handle how inferior he felt when he was near her. Jocelyn made everything around her brighter. Not only through her singing and acting on stage, but with her heart. Her smile. Her laugh. The way she fit in with his family. How humble and selfless she was.

She'd come from a less than stellar upbringing and instead of using that as a crutch, as an excuse, she made the best out of every situation without a complaint. Her setbacks seemed to make her stronger. Not once did she blame her foster families for her poverty, or her sister for her homelessness. Instead, she took on the extra responsibility of caring for her sister and her bills even though it left her nearly destitute.

Patrick couldn't say he'd have done the same. Sure, he would do anything for his family, but to come out on the other side with a bright and sunny disposition? No. He was a regular grump for no real reason other than his sisters inherited all the sunshine and roses mentality.

They'd kick him in the shins and his mother would read him the riot act for being so rude and dismissive to Jocelyn earlier this week. She wanted to see the lights in Portland. They couldn't compare to New York or Boston or any other more glamorous city, but that wasn't the point.

It was almost eleven by the time he got home from his evening shift. The downstairs lights to April and Jocelyn's place were off, but a faint glow shone in the upstairs guest bedroom. Jocelyn's.

When he got inside he didn't even wait to take his coat and shoes off before sending her an email. She'd been reluctant to give her email address to him the other day but without a phone, there was no other way to contact her.

If you haven't already been to Portland, I'm free Tuesday night and can take you.

He hit Send before he had time to second guess himself, which he was doing right now. Of course she'd already been to Portland. She'd asked him to go five days ago. He'd never told her he could go some other night so why would she wait around for him? And why would he think she'd even want to go with him now? Besides, she had her own car and didn't need him to *take* her. He'd been a jerk to her.

Stripping off his coat, boots, and holster, he padded across his dark living room to the kitchen and locked his weapon. He grabbed a jar of peanut butter and a loaf of bread and made a midnight snack. Not the healthiest of lifestyles. Tomorrow morning he'd put in a few miles on the treadmill before his shift. If his heavy panting slow jog with Jocelyn a few weeks ago was any indicator, he needed to spend more time on it anyway.

He took a bite of his sandwich and went upstairs to change into sweats. When he returned, his phone glowed indicating a new email. Picking it up, he couldn't help the tug at his lips when he saw who it was from.

Jocelyn.

Sure.

He waited for another email to pop up. Nope. That was it. *Sure.* Not *I'd love to* or *That sounds fun!*

One thing he'd learned growing up with three sisters was that *sure, fine,* and *whatever* were loaded words. Words that couldn't be interpreted through a hurried phone call or email and must be evaluated in person.

Not tonight. Tomorrow before she headed to the Playhouse. In the meantime, he finished in sandwich it two bites and chased it down with a glass of milk.

HER CAR WAS GONE BY the time Patrick woke up. He waited a few hours hoping she'd just gone to the store or an errand, but when noontime rolled around, he figured she wasn't coming home before she had to be at work.

It was just as well. Patrick hadn't thought about what he would say to her in person anyway. Asking her what she meant by the one-word response probably wasn't the best way to start a conversation. With no other choice, he waited for the days to pass, working his shifts and passing his free time away at the gym.

When Tuesday morning rolled around, he showered, shaved, ate a quick breakfast, and then picked up his phone to send Jocelyn an email.

He opened up their previous thread and winced. Sulking over her last message, he'd never responded to her *Sure*. Hopefully she hadn't thought he'd forgotten about her. This time he crafted his email in his head before typing it in a rush.

I'm looking forward to tonight. Would you like to go out to dinner first? My treat.

He hit send and winced again, closing his eyes in doubt. Would she misread the *My treat* as too casual? As an insult assuming she couldn't afford her own meal? Maybe she'd see it as a date, and if so, could she possibly be interested in him? Too many thoughts rushed through his mind. He'd been on the receiving end of his sisters' wrath too many times and knew all too well how women—some women—over-analyzed men's words.

His phone vibrated and he picked it up with an anxious stirring in his stomach.

Dinner sounds great. Meet you at the car at six?

Patrick let out the breath he hadn't realized he was holding.

Sounds good.

There. That was easy. He'd take her to dinner, have casual conversation, and then check out the lights in town. Nothing pushy or romantic about the evening at all. And yet, a string of hope wound around his heart and gave it a little squeeze.

"THE LIGHTS ARE SO ROMANTIC." Jocelyn tipped her head back and spun around in a slow circle in front of the Christmas tree in Portland Square. For the past twenty minutes he'd been enamored as she sang along with carolers stationed by the tree.

Her voice was that of an angel. Normally his taste of music leaned toward country and classic rock, but the sweet Christmas carols coming from Jocelyn stirred something deep inside him.

Patrick couldn't take his eyes off her. She had an innocent beauty about her. With her knit hat pulled down so low it kissed the tops of her eyebrows, and her fluffy purple scarf wound around her neck, the only part of her he could see were vulnerable eyes, rosy cheeks, and a big bright smile.

The Sugarplum Fairy ornament he bought her dangled from her finger in front of her, the lights from the Christmas tree reflecting off it. She hadn't stopped glowing since he'd surprised her with it after dinner. Her excitement was contagious, especially when she directed her sweet gaze at him.

"You were right. Portland is even prettier at night."

"It's no New York," he said before he could stop himself. Better for him to put down the city than her.

"You're right." She lifted her shoulders with a smile, the light from the tree dancing in the reflection in her eyes. "It isn't." She put the ornament back in the gift bag.

Patrick stuffed his hands in his coat pockets and lowered his gaze to his feet. Jocelyn surprised him by hooking her arm through his and leading him in a circle around the tree.

"Look around. What do you see?"

Obeying her order, he looked up to the top of the tree where a giant star sat. "A star."

"What else?"

Puffing out a sigh, he turned toward a side street. "People walking, shopping. I can hear carolers down the ways a bit."

"I smell a bakery too."

"Are you hungry?" They'd finished their meals of pasta and rich sauce not long ago, but he could always go for dessert.

"I wasn't until I smelled vanilla and cinnamon. This is what you can't get in New York."

"Vanilla and cinnamon? I'm sure there are hundreds more bakeries in the city then there are here."

"True. But it's hard to smell the fresh baked goods over all the congestion. There are thousands of restaurants smooshed together in such close proximity that you can't ever really enjoy or appreciate one at a time. And then there's the traffic and the smell of gasoline. Oh, and the cigarettes. Everywhere you go, you're walking through a cloud of smoke. Portland is so...clean. So fresh."

"Really?" He never would have called Portland fresh, not after living in Wilton Hills.

"Really. You have everything New York has, just not as much variety. It doesn't make Portland any less special. In fact, it makes it more special."

"But you always make New York sound so...glamorous. Like you're comparing our small state to the one city."

"I guess in a way I am."

"That's what I thought." He let his arm go limp in hers and stepped away from her.

"I'm sorry if I've given you the wrong impression about Portland, about...everything."

"It's not you, it's me."

She let out a humorless laugh. "I told myself I wouldn't push..." She shook her head and turned away from him.

"Told yourself you wouldn't push what?" Patrick couldn't make heads or tails out of their conversation.

"Nothing."

"Tell me."

"It's fine."

Oh, not those words. Not caring that he was risking putting his heart on the line, he put his hands on her shoulders and turned her so she faced him. "You're forgetting I grew up in a house with four women." And she had no stability. *Way to rub that in her face.* "I'm not the best at...this kind of thing. At saying the right things, but I don't want to be the guy who..."

"Who what?"

Patrick rubbed his jaw wondering how the heck he got down this rabbit hole. "I don't even know what we're almost arguing about."

"I said something to set you off. I'm sorry." Jocelyn matched his stance and stuck her gloved hands in her coat pockets. "I've been trying to...to not take advantage of your generosity."

He furrowed his brow in confusion. "Advantage?"

She nodded. "You're a very kind man. It's in your genes, in your blood, and even part of your job is to look after those in need. For this I'm forever grateful."

And here comes the rejection.

"I didn't mean to take your kindness for something else. I know you're just being gentlemanly."

"Gentlemanly?"

She nodded again, looking away from him.

"Liberty is the expert on twisting words and meanings around, but you may have her trumped here."

"That's what I've been trying to avoid. I know that your actions aren't anything more than—"

"Gentlemanly," he repeated.

It was now or never. Lay his heart on the line and risk being turned down by the woman he had fallen for or live with regret for never taking the chance.

"I need to be honest with you." He led her to a vacant bench. She sat and he joined her close enough so their knees brushed. "When I first took you under my wing a few weeks ago, yes, that was out of civil duty. The invite to my parents' place for Thanksgiving was a genuine act of kindness. I didn't want to leave you on the streets."

"And I appreciate your kindness, I really do. I'm sorry for thinking…" She shrugged again, as if her shoulder could speak the words for her.

Still unsure of her meaning, he continued. "You intrigued me that night. I watched how easily you fit in with my family. And then after your performance and when we went out for dinner, I was drawn into your story. Into you."

Those beautiful, innocent eyes lifted to him. "Thank you," she said shyly.

She shouldn't be thanking him. Obviously, he wasn't getting his point across. He took off one glove and stroked her cheek with his knuckles. "I've been jealous of New York."

"Jealous?" She cocked her head and squinted in confusion.

"I thought I was competing with it."

"I don't understand."

Out with it, fool. "I like you, Jocelyn Redding. I like you a lot and I don't like the thought of you liking New York and all its glamour better than being here." *With me.* "In Maine."

"You like me?"

"What's not to like?" He picked up a lock of her hair and rubbed it between his fingers. "Besides your obvious beauty, your heart is as big as your voice. You're smart, compassionate, fun, and charming. And I really hope you plan on staying in Maine—" *forever* "—for a while."

"I've been telling myself not to look into our time together. At first I thought it was out of pity—"

"Never. Never pity. I respect you."

"No one's ever said that to me before." She curled in her lips and blinked rapidly as tears welled in her eyes.

"Don't cry." He rubbed the pad of his thumb under her eye as his heart picked up its pace inside his chest.

"I don't know why I am."

"Is it something I said?"

Jocelyn laughed. "Yes. It's everything you said. No one has ever said such sweet words to me."

"You deserve them and so much more."

"Thank you," she whispered.

Hoping he wasn't moving too fast, he dropped his gaze to her mouth. He respected her too much to push her into anything she wasn't comfortable with. They'd danced around their words and feelings for too long. Now that his feelings were out in the open, he needed to lay out his intent as well.

"I'd like to kiss you. If you don't want me to, if you're not ready—"

Jocelyn reached for his hand. "I want very much for you to kiss me."

And so he did.

CHAPTER NINE

"Thank you for inviting me tonight." Jocelyn unplugged her flat iron and moved over so April could use the bathroom mirror.

"No need for a thank you. It's the church concert. Everyone in the world is invited."

"I know, but your family has been so kind to include me in your holiday celebrations."

April squirted a glob of toothpaste on her toothbrush and snorted. "And deal with the wrath of our brother? No thank you." She winked at Jocelyn before brushing her teeth.

For the past week Patrick had gone out of his way to spend time with her. Between his crazy schedule and her busy nights, they took advantage of quick lunches before she had to be at the Playhouse, or to grab coffee at a cafe near the station. He'd see the children's play, then go straight to work, and miss his mother singing in the choir.

They'd had such a wonderful week she hadn't wanted to risk their budding relationship by telling him about the amazing news she'd discovered in her inbox. It was like the stars were aligned to make her most magical holiday dreams come true.

Her prayers had been answered, only now she wasn't sure this was what she wanted anymore. In a matter of weeks, her goals and focus had done a complete one-eighty. She and Patrick had only known each other for only a few weeks and been dating for less time than that, so it was too soon to tell him how she felt, but she couldn't help the way her heart raced every time she received an email from him. And when he reached for her hand or stroked her cheek, fireworks seemed to explode all around her.

Love. It wasn't something she was looking for. It hadn't been any-where on her radar. Survival had been her one goal. That and keeping Kimmy's memory alive in her heart.

"Gah. It's the same look Noel used to have," April said as she spit into the sink and rinsed her mouth. "Who would've thunk our grumpy baby brother would be the next to fall in love."

"We're not...he's not..."

"Oh please." April wiped her mouth on the hand towel and rested her hip on the counter. "You are and he is and we all know it." She smiled and patted Jocelyn's shoulder. "And don't pretend you're not."

She brushed past Jocelyn and went downstairs.

Jocelyn went into her room to get her boots and padded down the stairs. "We haven't known each other that long." She slipped her feet into her boots and zipped them up.

"It took Noel and Ian three days to fall in love. And according to Ian, only twenty-four hours. I could say the same for my brother. We all noticed how he looked at you on Thanksgiving."

"Thanksgiving?" Jocelyn smoothed the skirt of her forest-green dress. "I was homeless and barely making ends meet." Last week, bond-ing over a bottle of wine, she'd shared her life story with April. Jocelyn didn't have much money in her bank account, but with the meals Patrick and his family provided for her, she'd saved a lot on her grocery budget and had wanted to pay April rent money.

April had refused to accept it even before she learned about Jo-celyn's homelessness. Still, Jocelyn tucked away as much cash that she could afford and kept it in an envelope for April.

"Remind me what your living condition and financial status have to do with love?"

April handed Jocelyn her coat. She slid her arms into the sleeves. Cocoa, noticing the coats and shoes, left the comfort of her dog bed, and shook herself before going to the front door.

Ignoring April's question, Jocelyn joined Cocoa. "Not tonight, sweetie. Mama will be home before you know it." She kissed the top of the dog's head and led her to the kitchen for a treat.

Cocoa caught the biscuit in the air and brought it back to her bed.

"Since you're not going to answer," April said, "I'll do it for you. Nothing. Absolutely nothing. You and Patrick make the perfect couple and I'm super happy for you two." She wrapped Jocelyn in a hug. "Now let's get going before my pregnant sister has a hissy fit because we're late."

Right on time, the doorbell rang.

"It's open," April called.

Patrick entered and closed the door behind him. When his gaze met Jocelyn's, an enormous smile curved his lips. She warmed in all the right places. He had a way of making her feel like the only one in the room. Like he hadn't seen her for months and she was a most welcome surprise.

"Seriously? Didn't you two go out for breakfast like five hours ago?"

"I know. It's been ages." He held out his hand. "If you toss me your keys, I can warm up your car. I'll stay here so I don't track snow through the living room."

Since Jocelyn had offered to drive, she dug her keys out of her purse and brought them over to Patrick.

"You look beautiful," he said, never taking his gaze from hers.

"I'm wearing a coat."

"I'm not complimenting your clothes, I'm complimenting *you*."

She shivered, not from the cold but from the intensity of his stare. From the adoration behind his eyes.

Patrick lifted his hand and brushed back her hair. "I wish I didn't have to work tonight."

"It's okay. We'll have fun for an hour or two at Noel and Ian's, and then at church. I'm sorry you have to work but Wilton Hills is safer with you on patrol."

Dinner at Noel's was loud, chaotic, and somehow relaxing at the same time. The Johnson siblings were a constant flurry of rushed conversation, laughs, practical jokes, and hugs. So many hugs.

For an hour or so she forgot about the turbulence in her chest, the guilt weighing on her shoulders from the email she'd received earlier. She'd become part of this family and their stories. Leaving them all would break her heart, but she had to follow her dreams.

After they filled up on finger foods and hot apple cider, they caravanned their way to church. Jocelyn found herself in a packed pew squished between Patrick and Liberty. The performance started with the children's group presenting a live Nativity scene, and the children's choir and the adult choir followed. Mrs. Johnson had a lovely voice, as did the choir as a whole.

After giving her hand a gentle squeeze, Patrick had quietly slipped out between performances. They couldn't say goodbye privately but he gazed long and deep, letting his beautiful dark eyes speak for him. She could practically feel his arms wrapped around her in the loving hug she knew he wanted to give.

Again, she got lost in the moment. Could she give up everything she worked so hard for to be with a man she'd only known for less than a month? In a few months, possibly a year, she might regret it and would resent Patrick.

Jocelyn had never attended church growing up and the thought of being in a church choir never entered her mind, but the melody of voices and the beautiful hymns brought a whole new meaning to the magic of Christmas.

After the service, everyone exchanged hugs in the parking lot.

"We'll see you tomorrow at three for baking, right." Mrs. Johnson scooped up Gabe for another hug. "How many types of cookies do you think we'll make?"

"More like how many cookies do you think Gabe will eat?" Ian ruffled his son's hair. "It's late, kiddo. Let's get going."

"You made a wonderful Wise Man," Jocelyn said to Gabe.

"It's the first time I've ever been in a play, and I wasn't even nervous."

"You're a natural."

"Do you think I could be in a play like yours?"

"They do children's theater in the summer. Maybe if you're still interested, I can put in a good word for you."

Not that she'd be around to see him perform. Her throat closed up and she stepped back, saying her goodnights with a touch of melancholy.

"Want to toss me the keys so I can warm up the car?" April held out her hand to Jocelyn. "I'm sure my brother will want to say goodnight without me lurking over your shoulder."

"Patrick?" She glanced around the parking lot and found his cruiser parked next to her car.

He crossed the lot to their little circle. "I was hoping to catch the tail end of your concert. Sorry, Mom."

"Honey. That was sweet of you. But I'm no fool. I highly doubt you raced back across town to hear your mother sing 'Silent Night.'" Mrs. Johnson gave him a hug and a gentle pat on his cheek. "Be safe."

"Always." He kissed him mother's cheek and shook his father's hand. "Drive safely."

"Keys? I don't want to be here while you two lovebirds say goodnight. *Again.*"

"We didn't get—"

"Easy." She held up her hand, warding off Patrick's excuses. "It's cute and gross and I may be a tiny bit jealous. Say goodnight to your girlfriend and then go catch some bad guys."

Jocelyn handed April the keys. Patrick's chuckle filled the space between them. "She can be a pest but at least she knows when to get lost," he said.

"Are you going to get in trouble for being here?"

"No need to worry about me." Even separated by their thick coats and gloves, she could still feel the warmth of his body. "Besides. I'm on patrol, which is why I can stay only a minute." He drew her into his embrace.

They stood like that, her head resting against his chest, his arms wrapped around her, and she basked in the comfort of his arms. She'd miss this. Miss Patrick. It wasn't fair to string him along, but dropping the ball before Christmas wasn't fair either.

She'd have to tell him tomorrow. In the meantime, she'd soak up every ounce of love he gave her and bottle it up for future weeks and months when she'd be all alone again.

Patrick kissed her cheek and dropped his arms from around her. He opened her car door and she climbed in and buckled up.

"Drive safely. Sweet dreams, Jocelyn."

"Hey, what am I? Chopped liver?" April called from the other side of the car.

He lowered himself so he could peek in the car. "You be safe too, little sis."

"Bah humbug to you too, Grinch."

With another chuckle, Patrick closed her door. Jocelyn watched as he crossed the parking lot to his cruiser.

"You make him happy," April said.

Another wave of guilt crept up her neck and wrapped itself around her throat. Loosening her scarf, she cleared her throat. "Your family makes him happy too."

"No, we frustrate him. You've turned him into a normal person. He's more at ease than he used to be."

She shouldn't pry but she couldn't help herself. "How did he used to be?" Jocelyn flicked on her blinker and turned right at the stop sign.

"I don't know. Moody. Libs and I usually drive him nuts with our obnoxious laughter. Lately, it doesn't seem to bother him as much. Funny. As a teen, he was the one who got in trouble the most. Basically, because of bad luck."

"Oh, do tell." Some lighthearted stories of Patrick would take her mind off breaking his heart.

"Anytime he tried sneaking out of the house, he'd either trip over something and make a crazy loud noise, or he'd forget he was being sneaky and turn all the lights on in the middle of the night. He was always bigger than the other guys. Something that complicated sneaking around. One time he got into a car accident. Nothing major, still, Mom and Dad got the call at two in the morning and had to pick him up from a party two towns over."

"Patrick was a partier? I can't even imagine." Jocelyn laughed.

"I know, right? So serious and stoic and now upholding the law. It's always the delinquents who turn to law enforcement."

"He was a—"

"Well, not really. I guess you could say he was a normal teen while the rest of us were semi-Goody-Two-Shoes. Except for Liberty. However, she never got caught with any of her antics. She knew how to sneak out of the house to go to a party without getting caught. But if you tell Mom or Dad, I'll deny I ever mentioned it."

"Her secret's safe with me. Promise." She pantomimed closing a zipper across her lips.

A few minutes later she parked in front of April's duplex and cut the engine. "I feel like having a cup of hot cocoa. Care to join me?"

"With extra whipped cream?"

"You know it." Jocelyn followed April up the steps.

Once inside, they changed into their pajamas while the water boiled. When Jocelyn came downstairs, April already had the mugs out as well as a bottle of crème de menthe. "I'm spiking mine. Want a shot in yours as well?"

"I'd love one."

When their spiked cocoas were ready, they each took an end of the couch and curled up with their favorite blankets. Cocoa hopped up and snuggled in her lap.

April blew into her mug. "So, tell me one of Jocelyn Redding's secrets."

"I don't have many to tell." Nothing except her sad and lonely childhood. She'd already told April about Kimmy and living in the foster system.

"What about boyfriend stories? You must have gotten close to a lot of guys working in the theater industry. And don't tell me they're all gay. I know that's far from the truth."

"One thing I love about the arts is the diversity. Gay, straight, transgender, black, white, Asian, Lebanese, it's endless. Everyone was accepted and had a role. It was nice."

"We're not as diverse in Maine. It's not because we don't want to be, it's just a very...white state. Ian's first wife's family was racist. They wouldn't accept Ian or Gabe because of their Puerto Rican background."

"You're kidding me?"

"Nope. Guess it worked in our favor because it brought him to Noel. Took him a bit to trust us, that we wouldn't judge him from growing up on what he'd been told was the wrong side of the tracks."

"I suppose I shouldn't be surprised. Even growing up in a diverse state like New York, I still saw my share of discrimination. I often felt guilty for being white, the privileged race."

"Yet you were a far cry from any privilege."

"Maybe. But being white often meant that my sister and I were placed more easily than others in a foster home."

"That's sad."

"It is."

When Jocelyn would have bouts of depression, all it would take was to see others who bounced from foster home to foster home simply because of the color of their skin, or because they had special needs. It kept her and Kimmy grounded and grateful for the few advantages they had.

"So, boyfriends?"

Thankful for the subject change—sort of—Jocelyn sipped her hot chocolate. "Not many. I went out on a handful of dates with guys, sure, but no one I'd ever call a boyfriend. This guy Andy was the closest to a boyfriend. We'd dated from time to time, but my focus had been more on my sister's care and my career, and Andy eventually gave up."

"I can't imagine losing one of my sisters." April poked a foot from under her blanket and rubbed Jocelyn's calf with it. "You're a strong woman, Jocelyn. I admire the heck out of you."

Would she still when Jocelyn told her the news? Jocelyn lowered her gaze and hid behind her steaming mug. The warm chocolate and hint of mint coated her throat and warmed her belly, but it wasn't enough to ward off the chills that crept up her spine when she thought about telling the Johnson family goodbye.

"Hey." April toed her calf again. "What's wrong?"

"Nothing," she said with a heavy sigh. Cocoa seemed to read her sadness and buried her nose in Jocelyn's hand.

"Not only am I a woman who has used that same word in the same manner, but I also have two sisters who've used it time and time again as well. Nothing means *something*. Spill." April set her mug on the floor and scooted closer. "I'm here for you not to judge you, I hope you know that."

"I do." Patrick may feel differently though.

"Because I'm from a nosy, tight-knit family and because I consider you a friend, I'm going to keep pushing. You really have no other choice than to spill. I may not have the right words or the answers but I'm a good listener. Sometimes that's all we need."

Jocelyn took another sip, called it liquid courage even if the alcohol content was quite low, and set her mug down as well. Wrapping herself tighter in the cocoon of her blanket, she leaned her cheek against the back cushion of the couch.

"I got an audition." And the timing couldn't have been more perfect, professionally speaking. Tina's voice was back and Jocelyn had been moved back to understudy. Personally, the timing couldn't be worse. She'd gotten the subbing job and her personal life had moved in a direction she'd never anticipated.

"Oh my word! That's awesome."

"Yeah."

"So why the sad tone?"

"It's in New York." Jocelyn closed her eyes and let her shoulders droop.

"Oh."

"Exactly."

"This is what you wanted though, right?"

"Yeah."

"I take it Patrick doesn't know yet."

"Nope."

April rubbed Jocelyn's arm. "If auditioning and being in that play makes you happy, you have to do it. My brother can be hard-headed, but he'd never want you to give up your dreams for him."

"I know."

"The question is, do you *want* to give up your dreams for him? Loving someone doesn't mean you have to sacrifice your hopes and dreams. If it's meant to be, it'll all work out."

"I suppose."

"Come here. Give me a hug. I'm going to need them more than ever if it means losing the best roommate I've ever had. And I'm not saying that as a guilt trip."

Jocelyn leaned into April's hug and sniffed away the tears that threatened to fall. Being smooshed between them, Cocoa wiggled her way off the couch and curled into a ball in her dog bed.

"I see many Johnson family road trips to the Big Apple to support our favorite Broadway star."

"If I get the part. And it's not exactly Broadway." But it was the closest she'd ever been. Working for director Stan Gagnon in his latest off-Broadway play would get her name and face in front of some very influential people.

"You're super talented. Don't cut yourself short. When's the audition?"

"The twelfth."

"As in the day-after-tomorrow twelfth or of January?" Jocelyn's shoulders slumped and she let out a sigh. "Wow. Okay. When do you leave?"

She broke away from April's hug and picked up her mug again. "My audition is at eleven in the morning so I'll be leaving early. Probably around three to allow some wiggle room for traffic and parking."

There was a fairly inexpensive lot north of the city where she could park and then take the train into Manhattan. She'd done it plenty of times when living in Albany.

"Okay." April sniffed and got up. "That means you need your beauty sleep. Rest those vocal cords and do what you need to do. And tell me what I can do."

"You're already doing it."

CHAPTER TEN

"You're what?" Patrick rubbed his eyes in disbelief. He'd only grabbed three hours of shut-eye this afternoon before coming to his parents' for their cookie baking party. He'd been too eager to spend the day with Jocelyn to waste more time on sleep.

"I'm leaving really early for an audition."

Yeah. He heard that part. "In New York," he repeated, having heard that part as well.

"Yes."

He should be elated, over the moon excited for her, but he couldn't fake enthusiasm. "It's for a big production, you said? A leading role?"

"Yes."

She didn't elaborate. Better that way. He didn't think he could handle listening to her ramble on in excitement about leaving him.

"Jocelyn! April just told us. We're so excited for you! When's the play? We're totally going on a sister trip to New York. Can you get us front-row seats?" Liberty barged her way between them and hugged Jocelyn tight. Something Patrick should have done.

"Sorry. She pried it from me." April joined them as well looking from Jocelyn to him. She quirked her eyebrow in that way only his sisters could do. It was something between an apology and *don't mess this up for her.*

Patrick lowered his gaze to Jocelyn's forced smile.

"It's okay." Jocelyn lifted her shoulder in a shrug. "I was about to tell her."

"When's your audition?"

"Tomorrow. Which is why I can't stay late tonight. I need to leave well before the sun even thinks about rising."

He didn't mind leaving his mother's cookie baking party early, but that was before, when he thought it was so Jocelyn and he could sneak off for some alone time. Now he'd have all the alone time in the world with her living over three hundred miles away.

"Oh. Wow." Liberty lifted her brows in surprise and gave Patrick a look identical to April's. "How long do you think you'll be gone?"

"I'm not sure. It depends on the time between callbacks and if I even make callbacks."

"And if you get a callback...then what? How long will you be in New York?"

Thankful his sisters asked the questions, Patrick stood outside the circle of women. He wasn't sure he'd be able to ask anything without her picking up on the disappointment, possibly anger, in his voice.

Jocelyn fidgeted with the blue scarf around her neck. "The play runs for three months and if it's as successful as most of Stan Gagnon's plays, there's always the possibility that it becomes a semi-permanent show."

"So, like, you'd move back to New York?"

"It's a long shot I'll even get a callback."

"Sorry to eavesdrop." Noel stepped into their circle, followed by Maria. "But I want in on the excitement as well. We're so happy for you." She hugged Jocelyn as did Maria, pushing Patrick farther out of the circle.

The loud chatter from the women should have put a smile on his face. Instead, he moved away from his sisters and Jocelyn and headed into the kitchen.

"You okay?" Hunter clapped a hand on his shoulder. "Couldn't help but overhear the news."

"Yeah. No. I'm fine. This is good. Jocelyn has an amazing talent. She deserves this."

"What about you two? You guys just started dating." Hunter offered him a beer from the fridge.

"No, thanks. I'm running on empty and have another long shift tomorrow." Patrick grabbed a soda instead, needing the caffeine. He could drink a pot of coffee and still sleep like the dead tonight, he was that exhausted. Only his racing mind most likely wouldn't let him have a moment of rest.

"How are you, honey?" His mother wrapped him in a warm hug, resting her head against his chest.

"Fine, Ma. The cookies look great." Better to turn the subject to safer ground. A topic that wouldn't betray the combustion of emotions swirling around in his head. Heck, his heart.

"Speaking of, your father can keep the grandkids entertained outside only for so long. I'm surprised they didn't run inside when you got here. They've been waiting to decorate the cut outs."

"They were out back sledding, so they didn't see me come in." When he'd arrived, he'd immediately pulled Jocelyn into the den to greet her with a hug and a kiss in private. And then she'd dropped the news. So much for making new memories on cookie-making night.

"You two will find a way to make it work," his mother said, squeezing him before lowering her arms.

He didn't need to ask what she was talking about or how she heard about it. His sisters loved to talk, and their family didn't keep secrets. It was too soon to have this conversation with his mother—with anyone. He kissed the top of her head and worked his way around the kitchen, taking the trays out of the cupboards and placing them around the table.

Like a well-orchestrated dance, his sisters joined him and Hunter as they set out the sprinkles, candies, and many colors of homemade frosting.

"I'll get Dad and the kids." Noel gave his arm a squeeze as she passed by.

April rubbed a hand across his back, and even Liberty kissed his cheek as they took turns washing up at the sink. Jocelyn kept her distance from him, literally and figuratively. Gabe barged inside through the back door along with a rush of cold air and enough snow to keep the food in the freezer cold for days.

"Bud. You need to kick the snow off your boots *before* you come inside." Ian rushed to his side and helped him peel off his layers.

"Sorry. The sprite is too quick for me." Patrick's father came in behind, covered from head to toe in snow as well.

"When I said you should enjoy the snow I didn't mean to bring the entire outdoors in with you," his mother teased.

They carried on the light-hearted banter while they decorated cookies, with Gabe and Georgia interrupting after every other cookie and asking if they could eat them. Part of him cringed with guilt for ignoring Jocelyn. Even though she sat by his side, he didn't have the courage to look at her or to hold her hand as he'd done through so many meals.

Not that he could have if he wanted to. She was covered from elbow to fingertip in green and red frosting and she couldn't be more adorable, even if there was a shadow of sadness filtering her light laughter.

He was a jerk for thinking about himself. Yet admitting how much it would hurt to lose her would make it harder on Jocelyn. That was the only slice of selflessness he had, giving her the encouragement and support to go back to New York to make all her dreams come true.

It would be selfish and inconsiderate of him to ask her to stay. Still, vocalizing his support was too hard. He'd tried to offer it twice during their decorating when everyone was buzzing about her audition, but the words got clogged in his throat. Instead, he sat there silently as he forced down the hot apple cider his mother had served.

Dish duty had never been his favorite chore, but he savored in it tonight. With Hunter and Ian at his elbows drying and putting the bowls, rubber spatulas, and decorating tips away, Patrick slowly and methodically washed each dish with care.

"You gonna be okay?" Hunter asked.

"Sure. Why not?"

"If it's any consolation," Ian added, "Jocelyn looks as torn up about it as you do."

"Don't know what you're talking about." He handed Ian the last frosting tip and scrubbed down the sink.

"Dude." Hunter swiped the sponge out of his hand and tossed it on the counter. "She thinks you're mad at her."

"I'm not mad at her," he lied. Hunter and Ian both stood in front of him, arms crossed, trapping him by the sink.

"She has that look," Ian said.

"What look?"

"That look a woman gives you when she's really excited about something and knows you don't feel the same. Maria gets this way when she plans a girls' weekend away and I'm stuck at home with Georgia who's been up every night teething and is a walking, crying gremlin. I know Maria needs some time away but, man. Sometimes I don't know if I can make it through the weekend without her."

"I was on the flipside a few weeks ago when you guys asked me to grab a beer after dinner. Noel hasn't been feeling great but she also knows how few friends I have and that I don't get out a lot. She wanted me to go but also wanted me home."

"And in the end, we compromised by picking up take out and having it at your house." Hunter lifted his chin toward Patrick. "Think you two can compromise in this situation?"

"I'm not moving to New York. I'd never survive in that kind of environment."

"What about trying a long-distance relationship for a bit?"

"Do you think you could've handled a long distance with Noel from Tennessee?"

"Daddy! Grandma and Grandpa said we can sample all the cookies as soon as you and Uncle Hunter and Uncle Patrick are done with the dishes."

"We're done, young Jedi." Hunter scooped up Gabe and tossed him over his shoulder. "Show me the goods."

Patrick followed his giggling nephew and brother into the living room where everyone crowded around a display of Christmas confections. Between bouts of decorating, they'd made thumbprint cookies, fudge, snowballs, and butterscotch candies.

His sisters and Jocelyn took up the couch, while his mother sat in her chair and his father leaned on the armrest of it.

Hunter, Maria, and Ian sat on the floor in front of the table filled with cookies. Patrick was left with the wall to lean against. It was better that way.

"Ian, take my spot." April got up, leaving the space next to Noel for her husband.

Liberty's lips quirked. "Paddy, you can have my seat." She patted the cushion next to Jocelyn.

It was a tight fit with the four women, but swapping two out for two men made things rather...uncomfortable. He wanted to be close to Jocelyn. To feel the brush of her thigh against his. To smell her flowery vanilla scent. To be the one she leaned on when she was sad or happy. Instead, he pulled a jerk move and sat on the arm of the couch.

If she hadn't dropped the bombshell on him earlier, he'd be planning ways for them to sneak off alone tonight. Instead, he was thinking about how to say goodbye.

Lost in his own thoughts, he missed most of the sampling, which was fine with him. He didn't think he could stomach anything stronger than cold water. His heart had been burned; water was the only thing to control the burning in his chest.

"It's getting late," Jocelyn said, scooching forward on the couch. "Thank you for inviting me tonight. I had a lot of fun."

"Hang tight, sweetie," said Patrick's mom. "Let me box up some treats for your road trip tomorrow."

Patrick stood as well and contemplated not walking her to her car. While his mother boxed up treats, the rest of his family treated her to a round of Johnson hugs and well wishes. He followed her to the coat closet, helping her into her coat before shrugging into his.

He didn't even bother turning to say goodnight to his family. They'd seen him surly before. Maybe not this surly, but they knew when to keep back. When the two of them reached her car, she set the box of cookies on the hood and turned to face him, an exhausted sigh escaping all too loudly from her lips.

They stood toe to toe but neither reached for the other. Jocelyn lifted her chin and blinked rapidly, finally resting her gaze on his. All sorts of emotions swirled around in those beautiful brown eyes. What bothered him the most was the fear.

The fear was his fault. This incredible, selfless woman had given up so much to take care of her younger sister and never, as far as he could tell, complained. She deserved all the happiness in the world. All the happiness, which meant taking the role in New York. And she was scared of his reaction.

Taking the high road, no matter how much it pained him to climb the hill to the top, he forced an apologetic smile. "I'm sorry for being a jerk, Jocelyn. I'm happy for you. You deserve this and all the other opportunities coming your way."

He reached for her hands and then gently pulled her into his arms. Resting his cheek on the top of her head, he sighed again. "I'm not going to lie. I'm going to miss you like crazy."

"I don't even know if I have the part yet." She sniffed into his chest.

"If not this one, the next one." He'd known her time in Maine, and with him, was limited.

"I wish I had as much confidence in myself as you do."

They held onto each other in silence. There were no other words to say. She was leaving and he was staying. A few moments later he drew back.

"Is it okay if I follow you home? To make sure you get there safely?"

"I was hoping you would."

The drive was too short. The walk to her front door was even shorter.

"Drink lots of coffee before you get on the road tomorrow." He kissed her gently on the lips. "Drive safely."

She hadn't said much about her schedule at his parents' house and answered only the questions his sisters fired away at her, but he read between the silence.

Only three actresses had auditions for the part, and whoever didn't get the lead role would most likely make the understudy positions. In a musical as big as this one, she'd said there were often two understudies, so chances were she wasn't coming back regardless of where she ranked.

"Am I supposed to say break a leg or is that not a thing?"

"You can say whatever you want."

Don't go.

"Good luck."

"Thank you, Patrick. For everything."

It wasn't until she was inside that he'd realized he never asked the most important question.

Are you coming back?

JOCELYN LAY IN HER hotel bed, still strange and unfamiliar even after sleeping here for the past week, the Sugarplum Fairy ornament dangling from one finger. Next to her on her pillow sat the snow globe of downtown Portland he bought her when they went to see the tree. Patrick had surprised her with it on the evening of her last show before Tina returned to the part. His gifts were simple and perfect.

The sentiment wasn't lost on her. He was proud of his home state and wanted Jocelyn to love it as much as he did. The excitement in his voice as he took her to some of southern Maine's most iconic tourist spots was addicting. She wanted to learn more about Maine, and discover and hear about it all from Patrick. But she couldn't do that very well from New York.

New York. The place she needed to be. She'd gotten the lead role even though she thought Chelsie's voice was stronger. Chelsie had more passion, being a New Yorker at heart. Two months ago, Jocelyn would've said the same about herself.

All had changed with one simple tap of a flashlight against her car window. One family dinner. One evening eating pizza and talking about her past. One walk around the cove. One trip to the lighthouse.

It wasn't one day or one moment that made her fall in love with Patrick, it was a series of *ones*. Even so, she'd met him only a month ago. She'd been dreaming about making it big on Broadway for over a decade.

If this was her big break, why did her chest feel so hollow and her heart wounded?

CHAPTER ELEVEN

"Man. Christmas is tomorrow. You can't show up at Mom and Dad's looking like this." Hunter panted as he ran on the treadmill next to Patrick's. "You'll scare the niece and nephew to death."

"I promise to take a shower and put on a nice shirt by then." Patrick cranked up the speed another notch, hoping his brother would take the hint and back off a little.

"When was the last time you talked to her?"

Nope. Hint not taken. But Hunter had never been known for his intuitiveness.

"Called Mom this morning." He picked up his phone and turned up the music. From the corner of his eye he could see Hunter's mouth moving. Patrick kept his gaze straight ahead at the television mounted on the wall, pretending to watch the morning news as he ran off his frustration.

No, it wasn't exactly frustration. Disappointment. With a touch of heartbrokenness.

The local news switched over to national news stationed in New York. The opening shots were of the tree in Rockefeller Center, to panning Macy's storefront, and then to an overly excited crowd smiling and shouting, hoping to be on television.

He couldn't help his eyes from searching the crowd, looking for her face.

Maybe it was more than a touch. It was a motherlode of heartbreak. His left calf cramped, reminding him he wasn't as young as he used to be, and he'd been beating up his body for the past twelve days since Jocelyn left. Ten mile runs when he hated running, over an hour a day lifting weights, little sleep, and fueling his body with coffee and microwave dinners.

The treadmill slowed, forcing his legs to a jog. Sweat dripped from his scalp and burned his eyes. Wiping it away with the back of his hand, he knocked the buds out of his ears.

"You didn't hear a word I said, did you?"

Patrick tilted his head and grinned at his brother. "Not a word. How was your run?"

"Fine. At least I'm not running from something."

"Neither am I." He wiped down the machine with a towel and tossed it in the bin by the door. "Hard to go anywhere on a treadmill."

"Paddy," Hunter called from behind him as he hurried to the locker room.

Instead of telling him to mind his own business like he wanted to do, Patrick waited for his brother to join him outside the locker room doors.

"I have to be at the station in fifteen minutes which gives me three minutes to shower and two minutes to get dressed."

"I'm worried about you. You've isolated yourself these past two weeks."

"I'm living the dream. You forget Chad and I went up north earlier this week. We put on four hundred miles on our sleds."

Snowmobiling along the Canadian border with a friend who knew nothing about Jocelyn had been the reprieve he'd needed. While he and Jocelyn had exchanged emails and brief phone calls the first few days she was gone, they'd become fewer and shorter as each day passed.

Being up north where it was impossible to catch a signal from a cell tower, and spending every daylight hour snowmobiling meant he didn't have to communicate with anyone. Not even Chad. He'd been home for all of three days and it was radio silence.

Out of sight out of mind, he figured. Not for him. Jocelyn ate up every inch of real estate in his head, but with all the real estate in the Big Apple, he figured there wasn't any room left for him.

Hunter gripped his shoulder and gave it a squeeze. "You and Jocelyn...you two look good together. The whole family adores her. If you think she's worth fighting for, then do it. Lots of people make long distance relationships work. In the end, if it's meant to be it'll all work out. If it doesn't, at least you know you gave it a shot."

"It's not that easy."

"You're afraid of getting hurt."

Too late.

"She's busy with this new play. I'm busy with work, as always. It was never meant to be."

"She's really a New Yorker?"

"Born and bred. I'm sure she enjoyed the little time she was here in Maine, but we don't have anything to offer her. At least nothing like New York can."

"If you're so sure about this, then why have you looked like death warmed over?"

"Because I just ran ten miles on a treadmill and had to listen to your annoying chops for the first six." Patrick gave his brother a light tap on the cheek and shoved the locker room door open.

After his shower, he skipped the shave and shoved himself into his uniform. Hunter had his chin tilted up as he finished knotting his tie.

"Tell Maria I said hi. I'll see you at Noel's birthday dinner tonight."

The way his brother made it sound, Patrick had been nursing a case of serious Jocelyn depression for ages. He'd known her for only a month, and yet she managed to fill a space in his heart he never realized existed.

There'd been other women in his life. Women he dated casually. One or two who had been more serious and meant something at the time. But he didn't remember feeling so...empty when those relation-ships ended.

Granted, he'd never thought about the future when he was with any of them. The here and now was all that had mattered.

Somehow a homeless woman with an adorable dog and a heart as big as the sun managed to strip away the monotony and boredom he'd never even realized he had in his life. Patrick had been living so much in the here and now that he'd never thought about the tomorrow. The what could be. The future.

Jocelyn Redding opened the door to all those possibilities. And in the process, opened the door to his heart as well.

"YOUR PITCH IS OFF, and the last time I checked, this song was one of reuniting with a long-lost love, so why do you sound like you're singing at someone's funeral?"

Jocelyn didn't blame Stan for the criticism. He was right. As the producer of the show, he had not only thousands of dollars on the line but his reputation as well.

"I'm sorry, Stan. You're right. I can do better." She rolled her shoulders back and breathed from her diaphragm before signaling the pianist to start again. This time, Jocelyn took a page from her former voice coach's book and pictured something that made her happy.

Carmen Lipinski had been like a mother to her, taking Jocelyn under her wing and coaching her for free when she had no money to pay for voice lessons or acting. Now, under the heat of the lights and Stan's watchful eye, she thought about Cocoa curled up in a ball at April's feet and hit her notes perfectly.

At Stan's nod of approval, she continued with the melody.

"'When I look into your eyes, the love I see can touch the sky. Your heart is as kind as can be, please, oh please, don't ever leave me,'" she sang. Like before, Patrick's stormy eyes filled her vision, and she hiccupped when she should have held her note.

"Stop. No. Again, the funeral, Jocelyn. What's going on?" Stan pulled up a stool next to her and signaled for the pianist to take five. "I need one hundred ten percent of you. We open in three days."

"I know. I'm sorry." It didn't matter that it was Christmas Eve morning. New York was a three-hundred-sixty-five-day operation.

"So you said before. I try not to pry into my actor's personal lives, but when it affects their performance, I feel obligated to ask. Boyfriend trouble?"

"No. There's no boyfriend."

"But there was."

"Not exactly. I'm sorry, Stan, really. This job means the world to me, and I'm honored to have earned the lead role. I promise not to let you down."

His bushy gray brows dipped low over his eyes, and his lips drooped into a frown. "You're not letting me down, Jocelyn. You were meant to be a star, and I'm excited to be the one to introduce you to Broadway. You've got the looks, the acting ability, and the voice. The complete package. All that's left is the heart."

"I have it in me. I promise."

He gave her a curt nod. "Grab a bite to eat." He stood and called out to the crew who were practicing off to the sides and behind the curtain. "We're taking twenty. Be ready to run through Act Three at ten o'clock sharp."

Jocelyn prayed twenty minutes would be enough time to wipe Patrick's disappointed eyes from her memory.

Doubtful she muttered on her way backstage. She'd been trying to erase the memory of his touch, of his kiss, for weeks, but it continued to play through her mind every day and night like a marathon of *A Christmas Story*. Twenty minutes sure wasn't going to cut it.

Once she made it to opening night and she had the excitement of the crowd, the lights, the wardrobe and makeup, Maine and the people in it would be only a distant memory.

Her dreams, her future was on the stage. That's what she'd always thought and believed in her heart.

Only now that she was living her dream, she couldn't help but question if what she thought she wanted her entire life was truly what was best for her.

"HAPPY BIRTHDAY, NOEL." Patrick wrapped his arms around his sister and squeezed. "In a few months, you'll be too big for me to do that." He looked down at her belly with a smirk.

"As if. I'll never be too big for a hug."

"Ha." Maria snorted from a stool at his mother's kitchen counter. "I thought the same when I was pregnant with Georgia. I can't imagine what it's like cooking two babies in there."

"Gee. Thanks." Noel smirked and rubbed her belly.

"You know I love you. Big belly and all." Maria looped an arm around Noel's expanding waist and pulled her close.

"And you're a brat, which must be why I love you as well. You're just like my sisters."

"We heard that." Carrying a bouquet of flowers, Liberty crossed the living room into the kitchen. "Happy birthday, sis."

"Lilies. I love them." Noel took the flowers and doled out hugs to the family members as they arrived.

It was loud and chaotic in his parents' house. As always. Whether they were kids, teenagers, or in their twenties, there was always noise. And when they started creeping into their thirties, the niece arrived, then Gabe, and soon twins, which would add more bodies and noise to their gatherings. The extra little people and noise were the perfect distraction to keep him from wallowing in his loss.

Since their work hours rarely meshed, he'd sent Jocelyn a few emails when she first left, wishing her luck. She'd replied that she'd gotten the lead role, and that her fifteen-hour days were long and exhausting, but exciting as well.

And then he was up north with limited cell service, the days grew longer in between emails until it'd been over a week and not a word from Jocelyn. She had a new life she was adjusting to. The last thing he wanted to do was interfere with it.

With the frenzy of Noel's birthday and then the excitement of Santa coming tonight, Patrick managed to spend a few hours with his family while avoiding the pity stares for being dumped by the greatest person to ever enter his life.

Which was the total truth.

When everyone started the process of cleaning up, he grabbed his coat and gave his sister one more hug. "Sorry I have to run. Duty calls. Happy birthday, kid." His early morning shift was a favor for Brent. Lately he'd been volunteering to work any shift he could grab.

"How convenient you have to leave just as we start doing the dishes. Typical Paddy move." April tossed a grape at his head.

"I'll do my share of dishes tomorrow."

"Your share plus today's share," Liberty whined. She was always the worst when it came to dish duty. Not that Patrick was great at it, but at least he didn't complain about it. Instead, he was the master of reasons why he *couldn't* do them.

"Give your brother a break. He has to go to work while we get to sit by the fire and sip our hot chocolate." His mother came to his rescue, resting a hand on his arm. "Will four o'clock be too soon? We want you to be able to sleep after working all night."

"Please. We're the one with a toddler at home. And Noel's got two beasts fighting for attention in her belly. He can sleep whenever he wants." Hunter grinned and draped an arm across Maria's shoulders. "We're the ones who need more shut-eye."

"Excuse me?" Maria pushed his arm away. "When was the last time you got up in the middle of the night? A marching band could come tearing through the house and you wouldn't stir."

"Busted." Liberty snapped him with a towel. "Help me with these dishes. Paddy and April can clean up tomorrow night."

Patrick left feeling better than he had a few hours ago. Working extra, especially at night, helped to keep his mind off New York. He was so tired when he got home thirteen hours later that not even the bright morning sun shining through his shades could keep his eyes open.

HE CRASHED HARD, AND before he was ready, his alarm went off telling him it was time for round two of the Johnson holiday madness. Dragging his body from his bed, he showered and contemplated not shaving.

The grizzly man staring back at him in the mirror perfectly reflected his mood of the past two weeks. He'd sometimes go a week in the winter without shaving. He often participated in the station's No Shave November fundraiser for different charities. On the first of December he couldn't shave the scruffy beard off fast enough. For whatever reason, he hadn't signed up this year.

A few days growth didn't bother him, but he wasn't a beard man. Studying his reflection in the mirror, Patrick ran a hand down his jowls and rubbed his chin. His mother would appreciate it if he cleaned up for Christmas dinner.

Eyeing the can of neglected shaving cream and his forgotten razor, he picked them up, sighed, then set them down again. Why bother? Maybe it was time for a new look. Last night Noel had told him his facial hair made him look broody. Standoffish. Since he had no desire to fake the warm and fuzzies and much preferred the attention to be on anyone but him, he left the bathroom and padded across the hall to his bedroom to get dressed for Christmas dinner.

Remembering the last holiday meal while he fought with the buttons on his light blue shirt, he stilled, then unbuttoned his shirt and tossed it in the corner of his room.

He'd worn the same shirt to Thanksgiving. The same night he met Jocelyn Redding and started to fall in love with her. At first it was keen interest. She intrigued him, the woman with beautiful, innocent eyes who was ashamed to be living in her car.

Her affection toward her dog and to his niece and nephew showed her gentle, caring nature. The way she so quickly and easily fit in with his sisters and their constant jabbing at him, and how she stepped in to offer her help to his mother had stirred something deep within. She fit in well with his family. Too well.

What he'd found the oddest was that it hadn't bothered him, hadn't scared him like the thought of making a commitment with any other woman had done over the past decade.

They'd sat close to one another at the table, her leg often brushing up against his, his shoulders bumping hers, as well as his elbow. No matter how much his parents ingrained good table manners in him, he couldn't help his size. Squeezing ten adults, a kid and a toddler around a table meant for eight resulted in close contact for everyone.

At one point during the meal he remembered Jocelyn tapping him lightly on the cuff of his shirt, asking him quietly where the bathroom was. Later that evening, she'd rested her hand on his forearm, thanking him for inviting her to his family's home.

It was ridiculous that a simple shirt could stir up so many feelings and emotions in him, especially when he wasn't a feelings and emotions kind of guy.

He had only a handful of nice shirts, and all were worn to holiday meals. Other than that, he was a T-shirt and sweatshirt kind of guy. Maybe by Easter he'd be ready to wear it again. In the meantime, he pulled his dark purple shirt off a hanger and buttoned it up, leaving the top button open.

Once he was dressed, he went downstairs and made himself a cup of coffee, not that he needed it. The noise from his family would keep him awake, he was sure. But it gave him something to do and offered a distraction while he waited until it was time to leave.

Had he been in a better mood, he'd be on the road already, but needing some time, he dropped to the kitchen stool and slouched over his cup of coffee. He stared off into space and thought about all he didn't have.

Jocelyn.

"REMEMBER WHEN WE GOT trapped here for Christmas, and Grandpa and Grandma and you and Aunt April and Aunt Liberty had to rescue us on snowmobiles?"

Patrick watched as Gabe spread an ungodly amount of green icing on a Christmas cookie. "I sure do. That's the first time we met you and your dad. I can't believe it was two years ago." Patrick swiped an angel cookie still sticky with icing and bit off its head.

He'd never understand why his mother insisted baking cookies so early in December. They were always gone before the holiday, which gave them an excuse to bake round two on Christmas Eve and continue decorating on Christmas Day.

"And then last year Mom and Dad got married. I wonder what cool stuff will happen this year? Dad says we've been blessed with a Christmas miracle every year since meeting Mom."

If only I believed in miracles. "Santa coming last night was pretty cool, don't you think?"

"Yeah. But he comes every year. Next Christmas I'll have a baby brother and a baby sister. I want something cool to happen *this* year."

So do I, kid. So do I.

"Um, excuse me? You don't think that ginormous Lego set I got you is wicked cool?" April took a seat next to Gabe and picked up a cookie and some frosting.

"I love it, Aunt April. It's cool but it's not like...like a miracle cool."

"Oh, I see what you're saying. So, something like your Uncle Patrick shaving that ugly beard off his face or maybe dancing a jig would be a miracle kind of coolness."

Brushing the crumbs off his shirt, he pretended to scowl at his giggling nephew. "I can easily take back the video game I got you and dance around like a fool if that's what you'd like."

"Do it, Gabe! I'll buy you another game," Liberty said as she joined them around the counter.

He'd better not call Patrick on his bluff. There was no way he'd do something as foolish as that in front of his family. Or strangers. Or anyone. Patrick was not the dancing or goofy kind of guy.

"Are you all ready to watch *It's A Wonderful Life?*" Since Gabe and Ian had joined their family two years ago, his mother had revived some of their family traditions that had fallen by the wayside as the kids got older.

One was to watch a classic Christmas movie after every family meal in December. Patrick had managed to make only yesterday's and today's, but from what he'd heard, Gabe had seen six movies so far this month.

The living room was crowded and in usual fashion, the women got the couches while Patrick, Ian, and Hunter took the floor. Uncomfortable on the hard surface, Patrick got up at every commercial to stand in the doorway between the living room and kitchen.

Halfway through the movie, Hunter was sound asleep, snoring like a bear. Patrick worked out the kinks in his back, stretched his legs, and stood. "Anyone need a refill on hot chocolate or cider?"

"Since you can't sit still for more than five minutes, I'll take a cup of hot chocolate. Extra marshmallows," Noel said, Gabe cuddled to her side. "And another cookie."

"Can I have another cookie too?"

"You better brush for a solid five minutes tonight, bud," Ian said from the floor. "And you might as well grab me one of Gabe's masterpieces as well."

"Hot co—" Man, he couldn't say it without thinking about her. "Hot chocolate, cookies for the Ramos family, anyone else?"

"While you're taking orders—" April yawned from her end of the couch— "another scoop of Mom's chocolate trifle would be good."

"I'll take some more hot cider."

"Trifle?" Hunter stirred from the floor. "Yeah, count me in."

Patrick sighed. His offer had been out of politeness since he was going to pour himself another cider.

"I'll help you, honey." His mother stood from her recliner.

"No, Mom. You've been on your feet all day. I got this."

"Need a hand, son?" his dad asked from his chair.

"All good, Dad."

Being alone in his parents' kitchen was a rarity. For the few moments he had, he enjoyed the soft murmur of the television from the other room and the uncharacteristic quiet from his family.

He scooped up a few bowls of trifle, arranged some cookies on a platter, added some of his father's favorite fudge, and carried the tray to the living room. "Beverages are almost ready."

In the twinkling of lights on the trees in the kitchen, living room, and front porch, the flickering television screen in the other room, and the glow from the fireplace, all was calm and cozy. Hard to believe how many people were crammed in the house at the moment.

Patrick leaned against the counter while he watched the pot of cider warm, and waited for the whistle from the tea kettle. Part of him envied the closeness of Hunter and Maria, of Noel and Ian, and of his parents.

While he'd always admired his parents' strong relationship, it wasn't something he'd ever sought. Not even when Hunter had announced he'd proposed to Maria. Not when Patrick gave the best man's speech at their wedding, or when he stood up front at the altar again to witness Noel and Ian's marriage.

Having his freedom, doing his job, and having his family there were the only things that mattered to him. He never felt alone. The Johnson family would never allow it. There were always family gatherings, meals to be shared, events to attend together. Not having a girlfriend meant that Patrick could actually have time to himself when he wasn't working or was with his family.

Only now those alone moments seemed to be more than they used to be. Or maybe it was the quality of his alone time. Instead of feeling relaxed and appreciating the quiet when he had it, he sensed something was missing.

The tea kettle whistled, and he made Noel's hot chocolate, then poured extra cups of cider because his mother and father would appreciate another cup. He loaded a serving tray with the mugs and carried it to the living room as a knock sounded on the front door.

"Anyone expecting company?" His father rose and answered the door. A moment later, he said, "Well, isn't this a lovely surprise."

Patrick couldn't see who was at the door but a loud bark and a whirl of tan fur barreled into the living room. Cocoa jumped up on Gabe's lap and licked his face.

"Cocoa!" Gabe giggled as he tried to hug the squirming dog.

"I'm sorry. I wasn't expecting her to take off. I had her on her leash." The apology could barely be heard over the giggles, but Patrick could pick out the sweet melody of Jocelyn's voice anywhere. He closed his eyes, hands clutching the tray as he tried to calm the racing in his chest.

"No apologies necessary. Come on in."

"I don't want to interrupt your holiday. I was hoping for a minute with...Patrick."

"Our Christmas is complete now that you're here. Come in, sweetheart."

When Patrick opened his eyes, he ignored the craned necks and raised eyebrows directed at him and kept his gaze on the tray, while pretending he had no idea who was at the door.

"Here's your hot chocolate. Let me know if you need more marshmallows." He handed Noel her mug, then served the rest of the drinks. "Anything else?"

The room was uncharacteristically quiet as they waited for Patrick to say something.

"Jocelyn. Merry Christmas, honey." His mother, who seemed to be the only one with manners, rose and enveloped her in a hug. "We're so happy you came by to see us."

"Hey, former roomie." April jumped to her feet and hugged Jocelyn as well. "How goes show business?"

"My turn." Liberty fought her way in, as did Noel, once she wiggled herself up from the couch, and then his brother and Ian even gave her a hug.

"I'd get up but I'm afraid to wake the princess and then you'd all see the wicked witch side of her," Maria said from the couch.

"Oh, please don't get up. I'm sorry to have disturbed you."

She still hadn't made eye contact with Patrick, not that he'd done anything to show his interest in her arrival. Holding the tray and using it as a shield in front of him, he finally looked her way.

"It's good...uh...nice to see you." The layer of snow on her hair was starting to melt, and he was tempted to reach out and brush away the drip on her cheek.

"And she brought Cocoa." Gabe giggled from the couch.

"I'm sure she's as equally excited to see you," Noel said with a chuckle.

"Looks like Cocoa missed him just as much."

The real question was, did Jocelyn miss Patrick as much as he missed her?

"I'm going to clean up the mess I made in the kitchen."

Like a coward, he spun around and left the room.

CHAPTER THIRTEEN

Jocelyn had never experienced such a churning in her stomach or weak, shaking limbs as she had now, staring at Patrick's retreating back. Not even during her audition for *Once and Again* two weeks ago.

"Shame on Alex for not taking your coat. Let me." Mrs. Johnson unzipped the front of her coat as if Jocelyn were a child needing help.

Her legs, heavy and stiff as concrete, refused to move, as did her arms. She stood there helplessly as Mrs. Johnson slid the coat off her.

"Thank you," Jocelyn whispered.

"Don't let him scare you. There may be scruff on his face, but his heart is as soft and gentle as a baby's. He misses you." She kissed Jocelyn's cheek and walked away with her coat.

The television show that had been paused started again, and she tilted her head to see what was on. *It's a Wonderful Life*. Fitting for this beautiful family. She could picture Patrick in George Bailey's role. All bark and no bite, and only when he didn't know what else what to do. Both were strong men who wanted nothing more than to protect the ones they love.

And both hurt easily, yet expressing their feelings wasn't something that came naturally. She wasn't a hundred percent sure how deep Patrick's feelings were for her, but he had to care about her a little or he wouldn't have been so upset with her leaving. Either way, she needed to speak from her heart or she'd regret it forever.

Thankful his family was now caught up in the movie—even if they were only pretending to be interested in it and not the drama that was about to take place in another room. She took in a deep, calming breath, and slipped into the kitchen.

Patrick's back was still to her as he tidied up, packing up cookies and goodies in containers and covering pies with tinfoil.

"Hi," she said—stupidly—behind him. "Do you need a hand?"

"No. I got it...thanks."

She stood in silence for a few minutes, as she watched Patrick work. When everything was put away, he turned from the fridge and acted surprised she was still there. While no lights were on, the tree in the corner emitted enough so they could see their way around the counter and table.

"When do you leave again?" His tone was harsh, almost accusatory. He folded his arms across his chest creating an imposing barrier between them and stood in between the counter and kitchen sink.

"I..." She dipped her head from side to side. Before she told him everything, she needed to know how he felt about her. "I've only been gone for two weeks. I had hoped we could stay friends."

It wasn't a long time, given they'd only known each other for three weeks before that. Yet both passages of time had a profound effect on her. It hadn't taken long for her to fall in love with him, and those two weeks apart seemed like an eternity.

She wanted his friendship—and more—even though anytime they talked or emailed, it reminded her of all she left behind. Their communication only lasted a few days before it completely ended. If she didn't mean anything to him, if she was only a charity case, or if this was just Patrick being Patrick, and she took his gestures as more than they were really meant to be, she'd feel like a fool for coming back to him.

And if she didn't tell him how she felt, she'd regret it for the rest of her life. He monopolized too much space in her head. In her heart. And it affected her performance on stage.

"Sure." He shrugged. "Just like you're friends with the rest of my family."

His sisters and Maria had called or emailed her regularly, keeping their messages short and about the kids or Noel's pregnancy. They asked a lot of questions and asked for pictures, never mentioning Patrick or asking about their relationship.

The lack of his name popping up in their group emails was either because "Jocelyn and Patrick" were over or because they respected her privacy. Ninety percent of the time she erred on the first. The Johnson sisters, and even Maria, were known for being nosy. Which only left a ten percent chance that there was ever anything real between her and Patrick.

"Can we talk?"

"I thought that's what we were doing." With his arms crossed and the unfamiliar beard, he didn't look or sound like the Patrick she loved.

She took a careful step closer, her arms dangling by her side. "I think about the times we spent together. A lot." *Too often.* "Our lunch-es. Our walk around the cove. Thanksgiving. You meant...you *mean* a lot to me, Patrick."

Even under the layer of facial hair, she could see the tic in his neck. He lowered his arms, tucking his hands in the front pockets of his khakis. "Thanks."

Her eyes stung. Her throat swelled up from the rejection. He didn't reciprocate. Clamping her lips so he wouldn't notice the tremble, she gave him a curt nod and turned to leave.

"Wait. Jocelyn."

Frozen in her tracks, she kept her back to him as she used her sweater cuff to wipe away her tears. She wouldn't turn, wouldn't say a word. It was a huge mistake coming here in the first place.

"Those days...the time we spent together meant a lot to me too."

The words he spoke were welcome, but too late. Too forced. They were from the Johnson Family Manners Handbook, not from his heart.

"I'll let you get back to your family and the movie." She took an-other step toward the living room.

"Why did you come back?" This time his tone wasn't harsh. If any-thing, he sounded vulnerable.

Slowly, she faced him again and sniffed. Patrick reached for a napkin and handed it to her. "You're crying."

"I'm okay." Another lie. She took the napkin and dabbed the corners of her eyes and then her nose. "If I ask you something do you promise to be one hundred percent honest with me? I don't want you to sugarcoat it or say what you think I want to hear to avoid hurting my feelings."

She almost laughed at the shock and fear that etched Patrick's face. "Okay."

"I mean it." Digging up all the courage she could muster, she rolled her shoulders back and tucked her tissue in her pocket. "You don't think I am, but I'm a strong woman. I don't need to be placated. Got it?" She pointed her finger at him. "Be a man and tell me the truth."

He opened his mouth but no words came out. Clamping his lips shut, he nodded.

Swallowing her pride, she propped her fists on her hips and looked him square in the face. Darn those soft, sensitive, and vulnerable eyes. Mustering up all her strength, she blurted out, "Do you like me? Like, *like* me like me? Not as a friend. Well, I hope you like me as a friend. I thought—think of you as one. But would you..." she lifted a hand, searching for the right words to say.

They didn't come so she continued to babble and swirled her hand in the air as if it would conjure up eloquence. "Would you date me? I mean, I thought that's what we were doing...before. And now, now I don't know what's going on." Not caring how unladylike she looked or sounded, she wiped her nose with the back of her hand. "Would you go out on a date with me again? Not to appease me or because you're being nice and feel bad for turning me down, but because you really want to go on a date with me? And then maybe another one? Could you see that happening? Because after a few dates it would turn into maybe a like, a girlfriend-boyfriend thing. But I don't know if you want that since you let go so easily. I want that and so I get why you'd need to say no to a date if you—"

Strong hands gripped hers and yanked her toward him. She thumped into Patrick's chest. "Yes."

She looked up at him and froze. His stare as intense as the burning in her chest.

"Yes?"

"I've been telling myself no because I thought the long-distance relationship would be too hard. But you know what's harder?" He pulled her into his embrace and lifted her chin with the tip of his finger. His words came out in a soft whisper that caressed her skin. "Not talking to you. Not seeing you. I've been miserable these past few weeks. I'll do whatever it takes to see you again."

"Really?" She could literally faint from her pulse racing through her body, sending a rush of blood from her head.

"Six hours is long, but three isn't that bad. I looked at halfway points. If I take 95 to New York we can meet in Rhode Island, tour the mansions, walk along the coast. Or I could take the Mass Pike and meet at the Nipmuck State Forest. I've never been but it's right off the interstate. We could go for a hike, walk around. Or meet up in Mystic, Connecticut. I've never been there either but I heard—"

"You looked up places for us to meet?" He shrugged. "When did you do that?"

"The night you left."

"Patrick." She lifted her hands to his face and cupped his cheeks, the covering of facial hair new to her. "You're a very sweet man."

He squinted, a sly grin tugging at his lip. "Sweet? You can't let that get out. My reputation will be completely ruined."

"I'm pretty sure this beard of yours is keeping your bad-boy image alive."

"You don't like it?" He placed his hand over hers and rubbed his beard.

"I didn't say that."

"I haven't had the energy or motivation to shave for the past few weeks." He mirrored her pose and cupped her cheeks in his palms. "I've missed you."

"I missed you too."

"Have you ever been to the mansions in Rhode Island? I don't know what your schedule is like, but maybe some morning we could meet there—"

"No. I don't think that's a good idea."

He dropped his hands and stepped back. Immediately, she missed the warmth from his body.

"I'm sorry. I guess I misunderstood."

"You did, but I didn't make myself clear." This time when she stepped into his space, the vibe was different. The spark of mischief and joy lit a fire in her, and she played out her teasing a little longer.

"Yeah. I'm confused even more than ever now." Patrick linked his hands on top of his head. His shirt tugged and pulled at the muscles in his chest and arms. "Are you saying you're interested in seeing where things will go between us or were you just wondering if that's where we would have been heading had you stayed in Maine?"

"Both."

"Clear as mud, Jocelyn. Do you want to meet in Rhode Island or don't you?" The tension in his voice was back and now she felt guilty for putting it there.

She sidled up to him and rested her hands on his chest. "I'd very much like to tour the mansions in Rhode Island with you, but I'd rather if we drove down together."

"Like tomorrow? When are you going back to New York?"

"Oh, did I forget to mention that?" She looped her arms around his neck. "I don't live in New York anymore. I was kind of hoping your sister still had my room available in her apartment."

Patrick's mouth fell open. He stared at her, the only movement coming from the occasional lowering of his lashes in slow blinks. "Your play?" he finally asked.

"It wasn't meant to be."

"You got the lead role."

"I did. It doesn't mean it was a right fit for me."

"You'll audition for another play."

"I don't need to. You see, I already found the right fit for me, and it's right here in Maine."

"You're going back to the playhouse?"

Jocelyn laughed and rolled her eyes. "Now I see what your sisters have been saying about you. Mentally a bit on the slow side."

"When you ladies talk in circles, it's hard to keep up."

To be fair, he was right. "*You're* my right fit, Patrick Evan Johnson."

"Me? But your dream was always to become a Broadway star."

"It was. And I had my almost-moment and you know what? I learned that being center stage didn't feel right anymore. It wasn't a forever goal."

"A forever goal, huh? What's your forever goal?"

"I don't know." She wrapped her arms tighter around him and lifted herself up on her tiptoes to kiss him. "You'll just have to stick around to find out."

Patrick smiled into her kiss as he held her tight in his embrace. The kiss was short and sweet since his family was just in the other room. He pulled away but kept her tight in his arms.

"Why didn't you tell me right away that you'd moved back?"

"I wanted—needed to know if you lo—if you liked me enough to take a chance on me even with the distance."

He lifted her chin again, tracing her lip with the pad of his thumb. "You had it right the first time. You wanted to know if I loved you. And if I did, if it would matter if you were in New York or here in Wilton Hills."

She swallowed her nervousness, even though she'd been fairly confident a minute ago that he did love her, she didn't want to force the words on him or from him.

"Have you come to a conclusion?" The dancing in his eyes could be from the lights from the Christmas tree or from the lightness inside him. She prayed for the latter.

"I came to my own conclusion about how I felt for you before tonight." She'd fallen for him weeks ago.

"I bet I can one-up you." Gone was the serious in his eyes and tone.

"What?" She snapped her head back in surprise.

"You go first."

"And you say your sisters and I talk in circles." She rolled her eyes at him.

"I'm not the most romantic guy, so I'm just going to come right out and say it. If you haven't figured it out already, I'm in love with you, Jocelyn."

Her cheeks should have split from her giant smile. "I love you too, Patrick. So much."

Instead of sealing their love with a kiss like a typical romance movie scene, he continued on as, well, as Patrick.

"When did you first realize it was love?" He dropped his arms to her lower back, still holding her flush against him.

Understanding set in. He thought he could one-up her as to who fell in love with the other first.

"Our trip to Portland. When you told me you looked up dog-friendly places for Cocoa. Seriously, the way to a woman's heart is through her dog."

He pecked her on the nose. "Interesting."

"What? You don't think I could have fallen in love with you so soon? That day was wonderful. It had to have meant something to you or you wouldn't have remembered the Sugarplum Fairy ornament."

"That day was memorable, and yes, I got you the ornament because our time was special to me as well. And I wanted to see the sparkle in your eyes again that shone when you saw her in the store window."

If she hadn't already been in love with him, that statement alone would have had her heart celebrating.

"So, when did you fall in love with me?" She played with the hair at his nape and gave him the stink-eye while wondering when he'd realized what they shared between them was love.

"You in that purple sweater that brought out the innocence in your eyes and the love you have for life in your cheeks. I couldn't get enough of your laughter, and every time you placed your hand on my arm, I felt like the luckiest guy in the world. The more I learned about your humble beginnings and the strength you built in fighting your way to where you are, the deeper my love for you ran."

Tears flooded her eyes as she listened to Patrick's poetic words.

"I never knew such goodness existed outside my family until you sat next to me at our family Thanksgiving table. I knew before pie was served that I'd never meet another woman like you. You stole a piece of my heart that day, and I've been in love with you ever since."

Jocelyn sniffed back her tears. "And you're a big fat liar. You said you weren't the romantic type."

"See what you do to me?" He placed a gentle kiss on her lips. "That means I win, right?" That charming gleam was back in his eyes.

"Look guys! It's a Christmas miracle! Uncle Patrick has a goofy smile."

They broke apart as Gabe raced into the kitchen, Cocoa at his heels. She scurried over to Patrick and jumped at his knees.

"Cocoa, no jumping."

"It's okay." Patrick knelt and scratched behind her ears. "You're a good girl. Did you miss us, huh?" He laughed when he got a face full of dog tongue.

Cocoa's tag wagged back and forth a million miles a minute before she finally scampered off with Gabe.

"Goofy smile, hm?" Liberty leaned against the door frame, April glued to her hip. "What's this Christmas miracle my nephew's all bouncy about?"

"None of your business." Patrick draped an arm around Jocelyn's waist and pulled her into his side. She rested her head on his chest, relaying a similar goofy smile, she was sure.

"How long are you here for?"

"I'm glad you asked, April. You see, I find myself in a similar predicament as the first time we met." She watched as April's brows furrowed in confusion and then lifted in surprise.

"You're looking for a roommate?"

"I sure am."

"What happened to New York?"

"New York was temporary. This—" she looked up at Patrick— "this is permanent."

"Like Gabe said, she's our Christmas miracle."

EPILOGUE

Jocelyn kissed the tip of Daisy's nose and set her down in her crib next to Alexander. They were the most adorable babies she'd ever seen. Not that she had much experience in the baby department. Continuing her mother's naming tradition, Noel had named her daughter after her birth-month's flower, the daisy. And Ian insisted on naming their son after Noel's father.

They were beautiful and sweet, and Jocelyn was thankful to be able to help out Noel when Ian had to work. The long-term substitute position had worked out well and Jocelyn discovered she loved working with children and sharing music with them, even more than being on stage.

It had never been fame and fortune that she sought. She'd realized she simply loved to sing, and living in New York meant working her way onto Broadway.

Since today was a teacher workshop day and she wasn't officially a teacher, she didn't have to go in and had told Noel she'd come by to help with the babies so she could have some quality time with Gabe. Hoping for an hour or two of escape, they left not long after Noel finished nursing the twins.

Asleep in their green and yellow elephant onesies, they were precious. Jocelyn could stare at them all day.

"Now that the babies are here and everything has settled down, can we get married?"

"What?" Jocelyn swung around, nearly bopping Patrick in the nose. "What are you doing here? You scared the life out of me."

"Impossible." He placed his hands on her hips and drew her into the circle of his arms. "There's plenty of life left in you. I can see it in your eyes, the way you look at those babies. You're a natural." He kissed the top of her head and then moved to the crib. "They're cute."

"Can we go back to what you said earlier?"

"That there's plenty of life left in you?"

"Patrick Evan Johnson." She stood with her hands on her hips and gave him the stern glare she'd learned from his mother and sisters.

That goofy smile Gabe had pointed out on Christmas took over his face on a daily basis now, and she loved him even more for it. He still spent a lot of time on the serious side, but every day brought more and more moments, like now, when he'd test her with his teasing.

"We don't want to wake the twins." Holding her hand, he led her down the hall and took the stairs to the back deck. The sun was bright and the air a comfortable seventy degrees. "With only a few weeks left of school we're going to have to adjust to a different schedule. Starring in the summer play at the Playhouse is going to keep you busy."

"And taking summer classes to earn my teaching degree, but that's not what you were talking about upstairs."

"It has something to do with it."

Her nerves couldn't handle much more. He'd basically said they were going to get married, but he hadn't proposed. Yet. Soon, maybe? Or was this part of what he meant by not being romantic? They'd just sort of talk about marriage and then make it happen.

Jocelyn wouldn't be disappointed. Having an elaborate engagement or even wedding wasn't something she thought much about. What she did daydream about was *being* married. To Patrick.

"You still haven't told me what you're doing here."

"And here I thought you'd be happy to see me."

"I think you enjoy testing my patience."

"It amuses my dad when he does the same to my mom."

Again, the marital reference.

"And you think someday we'll do the same?"

"I suppose." He lifted a shoulder as if he hadn't given it much thought.

Now that the twins are born, can we get married? She knew she heard him correctly upstairs. She may have been in baby euphoria, but her ears had not deceived her.

"You know those annoying traits you complain your sisters have?" She jabbed her finger into his chest. "You have them too."

She huffed out a sigh and turned to go inside.

"Not so fast, sweetheart." He looped an arm around her waist and tugged her back to him. "Come here." Taking her hand in his, he dragged her out onto the lawn.

"I didn't bring the monitor down. What if the twins wake up?"

Patrick pointed to the windows overlooking the backyard. "I've heard those minions screech. We'll hear them just fine. Besides, the back slider is open."

She opened her mouth to ask him what the heck was going on with him when she saw Cocoa run around the corner of the house. She barked and ran to them, rubbing her nose into Jocelyn's calves.

"Hey, girl. Where did you come from? I thought you were with April at the clinic?" She dropped to her knees and scratched behind Cocoa's ears. "Patrick, do you think—"

"I brought her with me." He drew her to her feet.

"I thought you were working." Only now she realized he wasn't in uniform. That wasn't uncommon. He often went to the gym before or after work, but he wasn't in gym clothes either.

She skimmed her hands down the buttons of his light blue shirt. "Patrick?"

He took her hands in his and then dropped to one knee. "Jocelyn."

"Oh." She tried to lift her hands to her face, but he held them firmly in his grasp. Her heart raced as she knew—hoped, prayed—what was coming next.

"I've told you a hundred times before, I'm no romantic, so I apologize in advance for blundering this. And I've also told you a thousand times before how much I love you. Normally I don't like to repeat myself, but those are three little words I plan on saying over and over and over again."

He paused, took in a deep breath, and then let it out in a quick huff. Her heart continued to race in her chest while she waited for him to finish.

"I never thought I wanted to settle down, to get married, and have kids, but the day I found you in the parking lot and brought you home to Thanksgiving, totally and completely flipped my world upside down. I couldn't think, couldn't focus on anything but you. When you left for New York, I felt my whole world shatter around me, and I didn't realize how much I had until I lost it. Lost you. I don't ever want to feel like that again. Lost. Alone. Without you. I know it's not really a fair deal. I don't have much to offer you and you give me so much, but if you can deal with my lack of romance and finesse, I'd be most honored if you'd be my wife."

"Oh, Patrick." She dropped to her knees before him, her face wet with tears.

"Shoot. That didn't come out anything like I'd practiced."

"It was perfect and beautiful and I love you even more for speaking from the heart."

He released her hands and cupped her face as he kissed away her tears of joy. "I love you, Jocelyn. I love your heart. Your inner beauty, your voice, your eyes, your ability to love and care for others. There are a million other reasons I love you, but I can't think straight right now. I promise though, I'll tell you what they are over the next fifty years. I want to have a family with you. Maybe start with a chocolate lab named Aladdin as a playmate for Cocoa. Whatever you want I'll give to you. Will you marry me?"

Touched by his words and even more that he remembered the story of the dog she and her sister had talked about getting, she blinked back her tears and leaned into his embrace. "I'll love you forever, Patrick, and would be most honored and humbled to marry you."

"You really are my Christmas miracle."

THE END

Acknowledgements:

Thank you, Kristina Sprague, for your enthusiastic ideas. Ian and Noel got their twins! I hope you approve of Jocelyn's name.

I hadn't planned on turning *Marshmallows & Mistletoe* into a series, but man, the peer pressure was strong! So, thank you to my readers who encouraged me to continue writing the Johnson sibling's love stories.

May the joy of the season spread merry and bright through you all, my dear reader friends.

Happy Holidays.

xoxo

Marianne

If you enjoyed Patrick and Jocelyn's love story, please consider leaving a review wherever you purchased the book. Reviews help spread the word to other readers!

I love hearing from my readers. You can email me at mariannericeauthor@gmail.com. I do my best to reply to every email within a reasonable amount of time.

You can read more about the Johnson family by checking out the first book in Marianne's Wilton Hills Christmas series:

Wilton Hills Christmas:[1]

Marshmallows & Mistletoe

Cocoa & Carols

Be sure to check out more books by Marianne Rice at: www.mariannerice.com/books[2]

Other series by Marianne Rice:

Well Paired series[3]

At First Blush

Where There's Hope

What Makes Us Stronger

Here With You

Finding Our Way Back

The McKay-Tucker Men:[4]

False Start

False Hope

False Impressions

The Wilde Sisters:[5]

Sweet on You (it's permafree!)

Then Came You

---

1. http://www.mariannerice.com/marshmallows--mistletoe.html

2. http://www.mariannerice.com/books

3. http://www.mariannerice.com/well-paired-novels.html

4. http://www.mariannerice.com/mckay-tucker-men.html

5. http://www.mariannerice.com/wilde-sisters.html

Wilde For You
<u>The Rocky Harbor Series:</u>[6]
Staying Grounded
Strawberry Kisses
Wounded Love
Playful Hearts

Dallas Firefighters:
Smoke & Pearls (free when you sign up for Marianne's newsletter at:
www.mariannerice.com[7])

---

6. http://www.mariannerice.com/rocky-harbor-series.html

7. http://www.mariannerice.com

Don't miss out!

Visit the website below and you can sign up to receive emails whenever Marianne Rice publishes a new book. There's no charge and no obligation.

https://books2read.com/r/B-A-LKSE-SJPBB

BOOKS 2 READ

Connecting independent readers to independent writers.

About the Author

Marianne Rice writes contemporary romantic fiction set in small New England towns. She loves high heels, reading romance, scarfing down dark chocolate, gulping wine, and Chris Hemsworth. Oh, and her husband and three children. You can follow her all over social media, and keep up to tabs with her latest releases on her website: www.mariannerice.com

Made in the USA
Middletown, DE
24 October 2023

41233343R10104